"That's What I Like About You, Fletcher—Not A Moment Of Self-Doubt."

"Oh, I've got a lot of doubts, Mrs. Daniels. One is that I doubt I can stop myself from kissing you right now."

"Fletcher—"

"You want me to?" He used one knuckle to lift her chin. "I want to kiss you very badly. I've wanted to all day." He caressed her throat then, drawing little whorling patterns with his thumb. "Haven't you felt the same way?"

"Maybe," Amelia whispered.

"A long kiss," Fletcher said, finding the spot on her throat where her pulse beat closest to the skin. "Nothing quick like this morning. I want a long, slow kiss from you, Amelia."

"We should exercise some self-control, Fletcher."

"Is that what you really want?"

Amelia closed her eyes to revel more completely in his caress. "You

"And you're cr

Dear Reader:

Welcome! You hold in your hand a Silhouette Desire – your ticket to a whole new world of reading pleasure.

As you might know, we are continuing the *Man of the Month* concept through to May 1991. In the upcoming year look for special men created by some of our most popular authors: Elizabeth Lowell, Annette Broadrick, Diana Palmer, Nancy Martin and Ann Major. We're sure you will find these intrepid males absolutely irresistible!

But Desire is more than the *Man of the Month*. Each and every book is a wonderful love story in which the emotional and sensual go hand-in-hand. A Silhouette Desire can be humorous or serious, but it will always be satisfying.

For more details please write to:

Jane Nicholls
Silhouette Books
PO Box 236
Thornton Road
Croydon
Surrey
CR9 3RU

NANCY MARTIN

SHOWDOWN

Silhouette Desire

Originally Published by Silhouette Books
a division of
Harlequin Enterprises Ltd.

First published in Great Britain in 1990 by Silhouette Books, Eton House, 18-24 Paradise Road, Richmond, Surrey TW9 1SR

© Nancy Martin 1990

Silhouette, Silhouette Desire and Colophon are Trade Marks of Harlequin Enterprises B.V.

ISBN 0 373 58015 0

22 – 9011

Made and printed in Great Britain

NANCY MARTIN

grew up in the Allegheny foothills and has settled there with her husband and two daughters after her years of travel. "My father is a pilot," she says, "and we were always hopping aboard small planes to fly over the mountains." She uses her experiences in the air to write about the flying Fletcher brothers, two dashing heroes who love their airplanes with all their hearts – until the right woman comes along! *Showdown* spells the end of Ross Fletcher's days of single parenthood and his brother, Abel, more than meets his match in *Ready, Willing and Abel,* both Silhouette Desires. Nancy has also written as Elissa Curry.

Other Silhouette Books by Nancy Martin

Silhouette Desire

Hit Man
A Living Legend

One

Ross Fletcher sat in his rusty swivel chair at the back of an old Quonset airplane hangar outside Missoula, Montana, guarding his plane from the bank repo man. With his boots propped on the cluttered desk, Stetson pulled down over his face, hands folded across his chest, he started to snooze.

But before he completely nodded off, Fletcher became aware of a female presence in the hangar. She hadn't spoken a word or made a sound, but he smelled her perfume. Strong and musky sweet, the smell took him back to the few memorable days of R&R he'd spent in the Far East at the age of nineteen.

But when he tipped his hat up with his forefinger and cracked open one eye, he didn't see an exotic Oriental woman in a skintight dress standing before him. Nor did he recognize the son of a bitch from the bank. He saw a skinny kid—no more than fifteen, he was sure—with a child's petulant face, yards of kinky blond hair and too much lipstick.

"Mister? Hey, mister?"

"I'm awake," he growled, struggling to get his feet on the floor and sit up. He groaned at the pain in his back. At forty-one, he was getting too old to sleep in chairs.

The kid backed off. "I didn't mean to scare you."

"Scare me? Hell, I heard you coming half a mile away. I have ears like a rottweiler."

Arrogant again, she flipped her flaxen hair behind her ears. "And a nose to match. What happened? You a boxer once or something?"

Fletcher glowered up at her and took a more careful inventory. Yep, she was jailbait, all right. Carrying a knapsack over one shoulder, wearing blue jeans and a sweatshirt from some snooty school in Massachusetts, she looked like a classic case of runaway blues. The bravado didn't fool Fletcher for a minute.

"What d'you want?" he asked. "You're interrupting my daily meditation."

For a moment, she looked as though she wasn't sure if he was serious or not. But then she regained her starlet's poise. "I need a plane ride," she said at last, resting her knapsack on the edge of his desk and jerking her head in the direction of Fletcher's aged Piper Cherokee parked in the hangar behind her. "You fly tourists around, right?"

He reached for the coffeepot on the windowsill behind the desk. "Sometimes. Depends on the tourists. You don't look like the usual kind."

She lifted her chin, playing at being brave. "I need a ride to my granddad's place, that's all. I can't get there by car 'cause it's up in the hills. Will you take me or not?"

"Not," he said, requiring no longer than one second to make up his mind. He poured himself some of the coffee that had been steaming by the window for hours.

Her eyes blazed. "How come you won't do it? I've got money, y'know."

"Enough to keep me out of jail for transporting children of the opposite sex who wear too much makeup?"

"I am not a child! And this isn't too much makeup. A lady did it for free in a department store."

"You didn't get a bargain." Fletcher put his feet back up on the desk and relaxed again. "You been hanging around shopping malls a lot lately?"

She shrugged, sullen. "Some."

"Getting enough to eat?"

She glared. "I've got money, I said."

"Yeah, yeah. What about school?"

She stuck out her chin rebelliously again. "I'm in college. We're on a semester break."

She was lying, but there was no way to prove it. "Hmm. Listen, honey, there's a storm coming through here today, so nobody's doing much flying. Why don't I buy you a soda pop and we'll talk a little while. You can tell me about college or how rotten your parents are. What do you say?"

She narrowed her eyes on him. "I know all about creeps, y'know. You better not try to lure me into that child prostitution stuff."

He grinned. "I thought you weren't a child."

"I'm not! I just—oh, drat." She looked closely into his face. "You're not going to help me, are you?"

"That depends on what you call help."

"I'll just hire somebody else," she snapped, snatching up the knapsack. "There are plenty of pilots around here."

"But none as good-looking as me."

Apparently she didn't believe him. Most of the women he'd met lately seemed to share her opinion. She stomped past the plane and slammed the door so hard the windows rattled. Fletcher sighed, took a gulp of coffee and nearly choked on it. He set the cup down again and went back to his sleeping position. It had been a long night.

Much later—judging by the new crick in his neck it had been about four hours—another female showed up. Only this one was more interesting.

She had high heels on, for starters, that clicked sharply as she stalked across the concrete floor of the hangar. And her perfume wasn't strong or musky, but rather a subtle mixture of scents that must have been blended especially to arrow directly into the correct gland deep in the male brain. Fletcher sat up and blinked before she said a word.

"I'm Amelia Daniels," she said, all business. "I'm looking for my daughter."

Amelia Daniels was a tall, willowy, blue-eyed, sun-streaked brunette. Her looks would have fit right in on the beach at Malibu. But her slim figure was encased in a no-nonsense business suit, the kind of expensive executive outfit that was seen in Montana about as often as Eskimos in mukluks—shoulder pads and a short skirt made of some pricey fabric. Her hair was tightly braided at the back of her head—classy. Her face had a stubborn chin, a determined set to her mouth and dark blue eyes that radiated intelligence, sharklike self-confidence and—at the moment—a flicker of desperation. Fletcher guessed her age as late-thirties, but she could have passed for younger in a different getup.

Like the kid who'd been around earlier, she seemed impervious to Fletcher's dashing good looks.

She said, "A man at the gas station across the street said he saw a girl come in here earlier. Was my daughter here?"

"I don't know," Fletcher drawled, mustering his most infectious grin. "Who's your daughter?"

"Her name is Zoe Daniels—"

"'Joey'?"

"*Zzz*-oe." The woman snapped open her handbag and flipped out a photograph—the kind schools take of every kid each year. "She's about five feet five inches tall, fourteen years old, wearing blue jeans—"

"And a sweatshirt," said Fletcher. "Yeah, I saw her."

Relief flooded the woman's face, loosening her expression. She dropped her gaze so he wouldn't see how deeply the news had affected her. Then she swallowed hard, took a breath and lifted her head, fixing those dark blue eyes on him again. "Do you know where she is now?"

Fletcher shook his head. "Nope."

"Are you sure?"

"Of course I'm sure."

"It's very important that I find her."

"I already said—"

The woman leaned over his desk, bracing her fists on the heap of papers there. "I have a right to know where my daughter is," she said, her voice crackling with hostility. "If you've taken her somewhere, buster, I'll see that you're arrested so fast you'll think a cyclone touched down and blew this dump off the map. Now talk, damn you, or—"

"Whoa, hold it!" Fletcher got to his feet. "Take it easy on the Humphrey Bogart routine, okay? I didn't take your daughter anywhere, but that doesn't mean she didn't get where she was going. There are half a dozen pilots like me in this neighborhood—''

"And I've been to all of them. That leaves you. Do I have to call the law to get the truth?''

Fletcher raised his hands as if she'd leveled a six-shooter at him. "She said she wanted to see her grandpa—that's the truth. I told her I wouldn't take her, so she—''

"Why wouldn't you take her?''

"Because,'' said Fletcher, "I figured some excited parent was going to come storming in here just the way you did, only I was expecting an outraged father. I don't have the energy for fisticuffs with Dad, if you get my meaning. Where is Dad, anyway?''

He couldn't help noticing that Amelia Daniels was not wearing a wedding ring.

She noticed the direction of his glance and looked very coldly at him. "That's none of your business, thank you very much.''

"You're welcome,'' he replied, taking no offense. "I'm Ross Fletcher. I figure your kid went to the guy next door. I heard his plane go up a few hours ago. He hasn't come back yet. What can I do to help?''

She looked at his extended hand warily, as if he were hiding one of those gadgets that gave the unsuspecting victims an electric shock. But Fletcher kept it stuck out there, and eventually she gave in, unwillingly polite. "I'm sorry I was rude,'' she said, taking his hand at last. "My daughter has—well, she—''

"She's run away?''

Amelia Daniels blew a sigh and put the photo back in her bag. "Yes, I guess that's what she's done. I can hardly believe it.''

"Kids," commiserated Fletcher, wagging his head. "They're a constant source of surprise. I have three boys myself."

"Congratulations," she said tartly, shooting another less-than-friendly look at him—one that sparkled with an unmistakable gleam of wry humor. "Do your boys ever run away?"

Fletcher grinned. "Now and then, but they come home when they get hungry."

"Zoe won't be getting hungry very soon. She borrowed one of my credit cards."

Fletcher would have called it stealing, but he didn't mention that. "How far have you chased her?"

She opened her handbag and began to rummage around inside it. "From New York City."

"The Big Apple?" Fletcher whistled. "I didn't peg you for a Manhattan type."

She pulled out a leatherbound checkbook and a gold ballpoint pen, ignoring his brilliant conversational gambit. "Zoe has come out here to see my father. He lives up on Tucker's Mountain. Do you know where that is?"

"Sure, it's— Say, you don't mean you're Brook Tucker's daughter, do you?"

Amelia Daniels's face tightened again, and she avoided his gaze. "Yes," she said shortly, and opened the checkbook. Pen poised, she asked, "What will you charge to take me up there today?"

"To Tucker's Mountain? Nothing."

"Nothing?" She looked up and blinked her beautiful eyes. They were blue as the deepest mountain pool at nightfall and surrounded by a fringe of velvety black lashes that weren't the creation of a makeup artist in a shopping mall. She said, "Look here, I'm perfectly willing to pay—"

"I mean I won't take you," Fletcher said. "Not today." He gestured toward the window. "Look at the weather blowing in from the north. Nobody's going to fly in a storm like that."

She studied the incoming clouds for a second. "That storm isn't here yet."

"There's no stopping it."

"I can leave immediately."

"Lady—"

"Are you afraid?" she interrupted bluntly.

"I've got two Purple Hearts that say I'm not afraid to fly in just about anything. My mama didn't raise a fool, that's all."

"If you won't take me, somebody else will."

He grinned. "Damn, I wish people would quit saying that."

Without another word, she stowed the checkbook and pen, shouldered her handbag again and spun around to leave.

"Hey," Fletcher said. When she kept walking toward the door, he called, "Hey, wait!"

She turned and looked at him coldly. A tall, sophisticated woman from New York City—except that her eyes were suddenly a little glassy, as though she were fighting back exhaustion. Or maybe tears. "Yes?"

She was a good-looking lady, all right, but that wasn't the only appeal Amelia Daniels had for Fletcher. Although she was trying very hard to act tough, Fletcher was willing to bet she wore cuddly flannel nightgowns to bed at night—soft, warm, girlish nightgowns that concealed a warm, very sexy woman underneath. He could sense it. In fact, he could actually see her in his mind's eye—that fine hair tumbling around her shoulders, her face alight with passion. Under different circumstances, the lovely Mrs. Daniels would be a woman worth knowing . . . worth having.

No doubt lots of guys pursued her—took her to fancy restaurants, sent her hothouse flowers for no reason, escorted her to the opera and gallery openings. But the wary intelligence Fletcher saw in her face told him she hadn't found the right guy yet—the one who understood her inside.

Fletcher heard himself saying, "All right, I'll take you."

Her expression didn't alter. "Why are you changing your mind?"

He couldn't stop himself from smiling. "Because no other pilot around here can fly safely in that weather, that's why. I'm the best. And because—oh, hell, I'm a sucker for lost kid stories, I guess."

She watched him another second, during which time Fletcher tried like hell to look respectable. She didn't look as if she believed his act, but she nodded anyway. "Okay, I'm out of options. Get the plane warmed up. I'll get my gear."

She headed for the door again, without a thank-you.

Watching her high-heeled exit, Fletcher called, "You have some jeans or something? You might want to change your clothes."

Over her shoulder, she said, "Don't worry about me, Mr. Fletcher."

Actually, he was more worried about himself. The man from the bank was expecting Fletcher to wait at the hangar so they could settle matters once and for all.

"But some things are more important than money," he said under his breath, grinning. Food, shelter and sex, for example. As he headed for the plane, whistling cheerfully, Fletcher wasn't thinking about food or shelter.

* * *

Amelia Daniels didn't think twice about the kind of man she was trusting to help her find Zoe. She thought only about how soon she might see her daughter again. But after she'd grabbed her canvas carryall from the trunk of her rental car and returned to the drafty hangar where the battered hulk of his airplane sat on the cracked concrete floor, she began to wonder. Maybe this Fletcher character wasn't the best pilot money could buy. And maybe his plane wasn't any prize, either.

He was pitching boxes into the belly of the small aircraft, working efficiently in the light of the open hangar door. A brisk breeze blew in, rattling the light body of the plane.

Amelia said, "You *do* know how to fly this thing, right?"

He flashed a crooked grin at her, hardly pausing in his working rhythm until he'd tossed the last box into the cargo hold. Then he passed an affectionate pat down the plane's smooth belly. "Sure do. This baby and I have been through a lot together. She's the number-one lady in my life—takes every order I give and turns in a top performance every time."

"One of those feminist-minded men, are you?"

He laughed. "Absolutely."

Amelia frowned, watching him gather up a few more things that were scattered across the hangar floor. She tried to decide if she'd better call him off. A flying cowboy was not what she'd had in mind.

What she ended up deciding as she watched him work, amazingly enough, was that Ross Fletcher was the kind of man Aretha Franklin meant when she sang about guys who wore their pants well.

He looked terrific. Amelia noticed at once that Fletcher was a man who should always wear blue jeans—especially tight, time-softened, slightly worn-out pairs that rode low on his lean hips and hugged the perfect, muscled contour of his behind. He had a *very* nice behind.

He also had strong shoulders, a powerful-looking chest and a face that—well, it could most kindly be described as rugged. He wasn't handsome exactly—a broken nose, lack of a recent shave and that ridiculous cowboy hat prevented that. But he was as astonishing a specimen of the male animal as Amelia had seen in a long time. Very tall, well muscled—efficient in a surprisingly sexy way. There weren't many real men in New York. At least, Amelia hadn't found any yet, and she'd lived there for fifteen years. But Ross Fletcher was real—not a pretty boy, but breathtakingly attractive.

It was a jolt to find herself thinking those kinds of thoughts when she'd been worried sick about Zoe for two days straight.

Fletcher turned and caught her staring at him, so Amelia hastily tried to compose her expression. His eyes were dark brown—almost black, in fact—yet full of sparkle. Had he guessed what she was thinking?

"Ready?" she asked briskly.

He glanced down her figure, dressed as it was in the same suit she'd worn the morning she'd realized Zoe was missing. His gaze lingered doubtfully on her shoes, most inappropriate for mountainous country. "I'm ready," he said. "But maybe you ought to change your clothes before we get started. There's a rest room across the street. Or if you're in a hurry, I'll just turn my back."

Amelia made a decision on the basis of the glimmer of amusement she saw in his dark eyes. "I have a feeling you'd peek."

"You're more of a temptation than my usual customer."

"I'll change later," she said, deciding to ignore that remark. "The sooner we get going the better."

"I can't talk you out of this? I hate to risk my plane—"

"I'll pay for any damages."

"Oh, yeah?" He looked amused. "And if we break our necks?"

"I'm ready to risk that. If you're chickening out—"

"You're jumpier than a long-tailed cat in a roomful of rocking chairs, aren't you? Just give me a minute to get the rest of this stuff inside."

The stuff, Amelia noted, was a couple of ancient-looking suitcases and a National guitar. She picked up the guitar to hurry him along. "You're not planning on serenading me while we're in the air, are you?"

"Hell, no, that belongs to my oldest, Jesse." He took the guitar and her carryall and pitched them into the hold.

"Jesse?" Sarcastically, she asked, "What are your other kids called? Wyatt and Billy?"

He slammed the hold closed and turned with the same megawatt grin as before, dusting his hands on his jeans. "Nope. Jake and Luke are the twins, they're fifteen. Jesse was supposed to start college this fall. Only he came home yesterday."

"A dropout?"

Fletcher took her arm with an easy familiarity, guiding Amelia around the wing of the plane and chatting as though they were old friends. "Yeah, well, I didn't want him to go in the first place, but he wouldn't listen. Now he's spent the tuition money, and we'll get that back when hell freezes over."

"Sounds like you have your hands full."

"Sometimes. You'll have a chance to decide for yourself."

"What? Why?"

"Because we have to fly into my ranch. It's the closest place to Tucker's Mountain since the lumber company tore out the airfield up that way."

"Hold it!" Amelia pulled her arm away from his grasp. "How far is your ranch from my father's place?"

"About thirty miles by horse."

"Thirty!" Amelia cursed. Things were getting more and more complicated. "You mean you can't take me directly to my father?"

"Nope. Like I said, that country's all torn up by the lumber people."

"Wait, that means Zoe might be at your ranch, too, right? The other pilot might have taken her there if it's the closest runway to my father's?"

"It's not a runway. It's an airstrip. But yes, there's a good chance she's been dropped off at my place. Most everybody knows you can borrow horses from me."

"Then what are we waiting for? Let's get started!"

"The customer is always right." Fletcher leaped lightly onto the wing, used the handholds on the fuselage to get his balance and turned to help her up. Smiling down at her, dark brows arched, black eyes sparkling, he extended his calloused hand. "Let's go, customer."

But something stopped Amelia from grasping his hand just then. She stared up at his face, wondering if she wasn't making a bad decision. Bluntly she asked, "Can I trust you, Fletcher?"

His grin widened. "Do you have a choice?"

No, she didn't. But the expression lurking in Fletcher's eyes was decidedly unsettling just the same. He had sex on his mind, and he was making no effort to hide it. Under most circumstances, Amelia could have squelched his hopes in a couple of sentences.

But in this case, Amelia found *herself* thinking about sex. Wild, laughing, fun sex—the kind that a carefree cowboy might provide. He was a randy, overgrown teenager himself, and in another situation, Amelia might have found that very appealing. He was probably the sort of man a woman could let down her guard with for a few days—a man who wouldn't ask for anything resembling a commitment because he liked his footloose life the way it was.

"Come on," he coaxed, his voice lilting with wickedness. "Time's awasting."

What choice did she have? Amelia shoved the brief erotic fantasy into the recesses of her mind, kicked off her high-heeled shoes and scooped them up into her arm. Grasping Fletcher's strong hand, she climbed onto the wing.

Fletcher slid into the plane first, and when they were both settled in the worn leather seats, he reached across Amelia to shut the door. Then he showed her how to buckle the safety restraint. When he seemed to linger over the task just a heartbeat too long, she pushed his hands away and finished the job herself.

Unperturbed but smiling, he flipped switches and tapped a dial or two. Soon the single engine spluttered and caught with a roar. After tossing his hat onto the back seat, he slipped a set of headphones over his ears and adjusted the microphone. His hair was dark brown with some flecks of gray showing around his temples. A widow's peak gave his face an arrogant, dangerous quality—like a turn-of-the-century bank robber.

He caught her looking at him and cast Amelia another grin—the kind that showed he didn't give a damn what he looked like because he was immensely pleased with himself otherwise. "All set?"

"Just tell me one thing, Fletcher. Am I going to have any more surprises before I find my daughter?"

He laughed. "Depends, I guess."

"On what?"

"On if she's met up with my Jesse by now, for one thing."

Over the roar of the engine, Amelia shouted, "What's that supposed to mean?"

"It means you could have a *real* big problem on your hands, that's what. Why, maybe Jesse's hijacked your little girl, taken her to the state line and married her! He's impulsive, you see. Like me, I guess. The boy's a prodigy."

"You're making me nervous, Fletcher."

"What can I say? You got to play the cards you're dealt, lady."

Grimly Amelia said, "I'll remember that."

He laughed again—a rollicking sound in the small plane. "You're gonna have lots to remember before this is over, lady!"

There was no chance for further conversation, since the engine began screaming like a jet on takeoff. Fletcher taxied the small aircraft out onto a rough landing strip he apparently shared with a few other small-time pilots. One burly man was pumping fuel into the tanks of another plane, and he lifted his hand to Fletcher. Fletcher waved back, but kept going to the end of the short runway. He turned the plane, spoke into the radio, and in a minute throttled back the revving engine.

"Here we go. Hold on tight!"

Amelia did as she was commanded and decided a prayer wouldn't hurt, either.

Fletcher got the plane off the ground after a series of jolting bumps and a loud backfire that caused a yelp of fear to escape Amelia's throat. Then suddenly they were soaring smoothly into the sky, leaving the lush green prairie far below. Fletcher banked the plane and headed west.

He flipped off his headset, apparently ready for conversation, and asked, "How long's your daughter been missing?"

"Two days," Amelia replied over the noise of the engine. She decided that even a mindless conversation was better than thinking about Fletcher's piloting skills. "She left a note for her roommate."

"Roommate?"

"At boarding school." Amelia sat back in the seat and tried to relax her taut shoulder muscles. "Zoe has—well, we've not been seeing eye to eye on the issue of school lately."

"You send your kid to boarding school?"

"Yes, of course."

He cast a puzzled frown at her. "She lives there, you mean? In some kind of dormitory?"

"That's what a boarding school is. She lives there and—"

"How old is she?"

"Fourteen."

Here comes the guilt trip, Amelia thought. She attempted to get a grip on her patience before she spoke. "Listen, Mr. Fletcher, I realize it's different for you out here in God's country. But you haven't any idea what it's like trying to educate a child in the city. It's a very tricky business. I decided that my best option was sending Zoe to a boarding school.''

''What was Zoe's best option?''

''Zoe is a child. She can't be expected to make difficult decisions like these.''

''She made the decision to run away. That must have been pretty difficult.''

Amelia laughed shortly. ''And look how she botched it!''

''I wouldn't call getting halfway across the country in two days botching it. She sounds like a pretty good survivor to me.''

Unable to keep the bitterness from her voice, Amelia said, ''Too bad she didn't put some of those survival skills to good use in school.''

''Maybe she didn't want to leave home.''

''I'm sure she didn't.''

Fletcher glanced her way again. ''So why'd you make her go?''

Amelia ground her back teeth. ''How I choose to raise my daughter is hardly a matter to concern you, Mr. Fletcher.''

''Sure it is! I've put my plane—not to mention my own personal safety—in jeopardy for this kid. As I see it, that gives me the right to know what's going on, at least. If your kid was so unhappy at school, why'd you make her keep going?''

''I didn't *know* she was unhappy,'' Amelia snapped. ''Every girl gets a little upset during the first few months, but I didn't imagine she felt as strongly about it as—''

Fletcher interrupted. "Let me get this straight. You sent her away from home and didn't even try to find out how she was doing once she got there?"

"Now look! You don't know a thing about our lives, so don't make judgments, all right? Apparently you're not exactly the greatest parent since Ward Cleaver, so—"

"My boys are doing just fine."

"But your oldest son just dropped out of college."

"So what? He didn't belong there in the first place. He'll find what he wants eventually."

"In the meantime, he ought to be in school. A good education never hurt anyone."

"Says who? Some kids don't belong in stuffy, regimented situations where all kinds of worthless garbage is forced down their throats by ivory-tower wimps who—"

"Does your wife take such a relaxed view of our country's system of education?"

"Ex-wife," he shot back. "She practically lives on Rodeo Drive now and couldn't give a damn what any of the boys are doing. She sells stupid-looking jewelry and spends her spare time shopping."

"Aha!"

"Aha?" He shot her a suspicious frown. "What does that mean?"

"Nothing. Except maybe you're allowing your own predicament to cloud your opinion of mine."

"Speak English, please."

"Your feelings about mothers in general are clearly clouding your opinion about my situation, so— Oh, Lord, why am I arguing with you? It's obvious we don't have the same views on parenthood."

"You've got that right!"

"We have nothing further to say on the subject."

"Except that I think *you* botched things with your daughter and now you're going off half-cocked to—"

"This conversation is over, Mr. Fletcher."

"I—"

"I'm not asking for your opinion on this subject!"

Amelia stole a look at him and saw his jaw flex. He was glowering—perhaps concentrating on the job of flying into a bank of roiling black clouds.

Amelia allowed two full minutes to tick by while she mulled over the injustice of parenthood. At last she couldn't stop herself from bursting out, "Okay, what would you have done in my place?"

"What?"

"Our situations aren't very different. I'm prepared to be open-minded about this. Both our children quit school. What did you say to your son when he got home?"

"Nothing," Fletcher said shortly.

"Nothing?"

"Well, I told him he had to walk home."

"What? That was supposed to be some kind of punishment?"

"Not exactly. I had things to do last night. I didn't have time to fly him home, so he had to walk from town."

"How far is that?"

Calmly Fletcher said, "Forty-two miles, last I remember."

"Forty...!" Amelia stared at him, aghast. "You forced a child to walk all that way? Alone? It must have taken him hours!"

"A day if he hustled. And he's not a child. He's eighteen years old and almost as big as I am. The exercise wouldn't kill him. Besides, he needed some time to think.

We're never going to see a penny of that tuition money again, and believe me, I could have used it a dozen times over. I could strangle him for that!''

Amelia laughed. ''Well, it certainly sounds like *you're* a model family! Maybe I'll pick up a few pointers while I'm in the neighborhood.''

Amazingly he began to laugh, too. ''Well, open up your notebook, lady, 'cause here we are.''

Amelia looked through the windshield. Raindrops began to streak the glass, but she could see grassy foothills below.

Humming to himself, Fletcher guided the plane lower, until they burst through the low-hanging cloud cover to skim low over the fields. A herd of cattle scattered at the noise of the engine. Amelia saw several dozen white-faced Herefords gallop clumsily away from the plane.

In another minute, she saw the ranch come into view, and sat forward in her seat to get a better look. The buildings were nestled at the apex of a triangularly shaped valley sided by two sprawling, snowcapped ridges of the Bitterroot Mountains. A picturesque barn, low roofed and painted red at least a decade ago, was the center from which several miles of crooked, hand-hewn fence stretched like the wandering legs of a gigantic spider. A few more cattle grazed near the barn.

It was a scene Amelia knew very well, indeed. But seeing the familiar landscape after so many years of living in the canyons of New York, she felt no warm tug of affection for the mountains. Rather, Amelia felt her heart begin to skip and skitter with an emotion a little like dread.

Set in a grove of trees was a rambling clapboard house with three gables and a lopsided porch that wrapped around all four sides of the building. It was picturesque, all right. But Amelia knew what reality lay behind the pretty countryside, the picture-book house and barn. Hard work and heartache. Not to mention loneliness. It had been the kind of loneliness a young girl hated so deeply she had once vowed never to return.

But here she was. And the land hadn't changed. Perhaps nothing else had, either.

Get Zoe and get back to New York, Amelia commanded herself. There was no reason to linger. No purpose in trying to settle things with the old man who'd kept her a prisoner for so long.

"Home, sweet home," said Fletcher, interrupting her thoughts with a crow of pleasure. "Hang on to your hat, Mrs. Daniels. We're going down."

The small plane thumped down onto a bumpy dirt airstrip and roared its complaint at having to stop before ramming the barn. Fletcher seemed unperturbed by the violence of the landing. He pulled the plane along the fence and cut the engine.

Amelia managed to unlatch the door herself, and she climbed out onto the wing first. The wind snatched at her hair.

From the house she heard a shout, and in a moment a teenage boy came loping into view. He was tall and stringy, wearing a beaten cowboy hat and jeans. Behind him bounded a mixed-breed dog—collie mostly—that barked at Amelia as she jumped down from the plane's wing.

The boy spotted her at last and stumbled to a stop. He stared, snatching his hat off his head but not able to force a single word out of his throat. Apparently he had never before laid eyes on a woman in a business suit.

Fletcher vaulted down from the wing and landed lightly beside Amelia.

Still staring, the boy said, "Wow, Dad. That was fast work. Did you marry her and everything?"

Two

———

"Marry who?" Amelia demanded, looking as if someone had just plugged her into a light socket.

"Shut up, Luke," said Fletcher, determined not to be humiliated. He slipped his Stetson back on his head to keep the rain off. "This is Mrs. Daniels."

"Yeah? Is she rich? Just like you said?"

Amelia swung on Fletcher, thunder on her brow. "What's going on here?"

"Nothing," said Fletcher. "He's crazy, that's all. Didn't I tell you I had a crazy kid?"

Her blue eyes were blazing. "Have you brought me up here for some disgusting reason, Fletcher?"

"I brought you up here because you asked so nicely! Luke, keep your trap shut for five minutes and take some of this luggage down to the house."

"Yes, sir."

The rain had started to splash down around them in fat drops, so Fletcher unlocked the hold of the plane and began rooting in the assorted cargo for Amelia's bag. The dog, delighted to see him, was getting in the way. Fletcher shoved the panting beast aside. "Where's your brother? Jesse can get his own gear out of here. I'm not going to lug it any farther than I already have."

"Uh, that's going to be a little problem, Dad."

Fletcher stood up and faced the boy, his fatherly instincts suddenly alive. "What's wrong?"

Luke looked at his feet. "It's Jess. He—well, you see—"

"Spit it out."

Hearing his master's tone, the dog flattened his ears and slunk under the plane.

"Jess got home this morning," Luke said in a rush, "but he took off again."

"For where?"

"Well, there was this girl, you see, and—"

"Zoe?" Amelia started forward. "Is she still here?"

Luke looked from Fletcher to Amelia and back again. "Uh, not exactly. That other pilot from town brought her up here because it was the closest place he could land. It was a pretty terrible landing, too, if you ask me. It was Miller, that guy who drinks. But—"

"He *drinks*?"

"Cut to the chase," Fletcher said curtly.

Luke nodded. "She said she had to get to Tucker's Mountain right away—"

Amelia cried, "Where is she?"

"Let him finish," Fletcher commanded.

Luke cleared his throat. "I told Jess not to do anything till you got here, but he said—"

"What did he do?"

"What could he do? She went nuts—screaming and hitting at him. So he took her up there. They left a couple of hours ago."

Fletcher cursed, spinning around to pace angrily in the rain. "What the hell was he thinking of? They'll have to spend the night in this storm and—"

"Jess tried to talk her out of it," Luke said, jumping somewhat weakly to his brother's defense. "He told her they'd be better off waiting till morning, but the girl said she had to leave right away. She wouldn't take no for an answer."

"Heredity," Fletcher snapped, glowering at Amelia.

"See here . . . !" she began.

But he overrode her protest with a burst of anger. "All I see is a pair of women who have managed to bully their way—"

"I did not bully you! I have every intention of paying you for your services, Mr. Fletcher."

"Damn right," he said, feeling mean. Jesse—the idiot! What was the kid thinking of? Probably volunteering to help Zoe just to make everybody think he was a man.

"I'll write you a check this minute," Amelia was saying, "if you'll add up the cost of the plane and a horse and some supplies. I want to leave immediately, so—"

Fletcher came to his senses. "Hold it. You're not going to go tearing after them."

"I have come all the way from New York, and I'm just a few hours from finding my daughter. Of course I'm going!" Amelia turned to Luke, who stood listening to their exchange and getting wetter by the minute. "Young man, would you please saddle me a—"

"Now just a damn minute," Fletcher said. "Look at that sky. Does the word *lightning* mean anything to you?

Downpour? Torrential *flooding*? The trail to Tucker's Mountain will be completely impassable once this rain gets started.''

"All the more reason to get started right away. Zoe may be in trouble or hurt and I—''

"She won't be hurt,'' Fletcher said, forcing himself to calm down. No sense alarming her more than she was already. "Jesse knows that much, at least. He's gotten her above the dangerous places by now. They'll reach the base camp by nightfall and—''

Amelia exploded. "That's supposed to comfort me? My impressionable daughter spending the night with your derelict son? Zoe has never been alone with a boy in her entire life—let alone a—a dropout! She—''

Fletcher laughed rudely. "C'mon, Mom, how naive can you be?''

"It's true! I've made sure—''

Fletcher stuck his face down to her level. "You haven't any idea what she's been up to. Once she got imprisoned in that snooty school, you gave up all rights to—''

"'Imprisoned'!''

"Hey,'' Luke interrupted, shifting from one foot to the other and jiggling Amelia's carryon bag. "Would you guys mind if I got in out of the rain?''

The rain had begun, all right. It was pouring down around them in buckets. Fletcher could feel the dampness soaking his shirt already, and Amelia's hair was shining with water.

A crack of lightning split the sky, and an instant later a horrendous crash of thunder rent the air. Amelia instinctively clapped her hands over her ears.

Fletcher flinched, too, but he had the presence of mind to grab Amelia's elbow and steer her around the nose of the plane. He gave her a push to send her after Luke, who was dashing toward the house. She obeyed without a second look back, and ran for the house as fast as her high heels allowed.

Fletcher stayed behind to tie down the airplane and grab two of Jesse's boxes. When he arrived on the porch, he was soaked to the skin. Amelia stood there impatiently, hugging herself.

Fletcher chucked her under the chin. "Well, Mrs. Daniels, ain't parenthood grand?"

"Look, Fletcher," she said, clearly holding fast to every ounce of self control. "I absolutely must find my daughter as soon as possible. I'm not joking. She's not accustomed to country like this."

Fletcher threw the boxes onto the porch. "She'll be okay."

"She could be hurt—she might be in danger—"

Fletcher put his arm around Amelia's shoulder. It was an instinctive gesture on his part, and he felt her start with surprise. He held her fast. "I know you're worried. I would be, too. But she's not going to get hurt. She's probably having the adventure of her life."

"She's never ridden a horse before."

Fletcher steered her toward the door, hugging Amelia to his side and liking the feel of her against him. "Jesse found her a gentle mount, I'm sure. Look, we'll go out first thing in the morning."

"That's too long! I can't—"

"You haven't got a choice," Fletcher argued. "You can't fight city hall or Mother Nature. Every cloud has a silver lining, Mrs. Daniels. You're just going to have to sit back and enjoy a little Fletcher-style hospitality for a while."

"One more cliché and I think I'll start planning your murder."

"Ah," said Fletcher, guiding her into the house. "Here's the rest of my charming family."

Amelia hated giving up. Zoe was so close—yet still too far away. Amelia's throat felt tight with the longing to see her daughter again. She didn't feel up to meeting Fletcher's sons.

As they stepped over the threshold of the house, two figures lunged at each other. Amelia blinked, and her eyes became accustomed to the dusky light in time to see a tall furious boy throw a wild punch at Luke's jaw. With a yelp, Luke staggered back into a ladder-back chair that promptly smashed into splinters at the force of the blow.

"Dammit, Jake," Fletcher shouted, "that was the last decent chair in the whole house!"

At the sound of their father's thundering voice, both boys scrambled to their feet and snapped to attention, panting breathlessly. Obviously, they'd been fighting for several minutes.

"What the hell is this?" Fletcher demanded. "I'm gone for less than twenty-four hours and you two start breaking up the furniture? Jake, you're going to mend that chair, you hear me?"

The boy, clearly Luke's twin brother, stepped forward. A splotch of blood decorated the front of the ripped football shirt he wore, but he didn't seem to mind that he had a nose bleed. "Sorry, Dad. We were just having a little fun."

"You couldn't have a little fun without breaking the furniture? Luke, what have you got to say for yourself?"

The boy, still boiling with anger, said only, "Jake started it."

Jake laughed. "I did not!"

"Did, too!"

"Did *not*!"

Fletcher managed to wedge himself between his two sons before the punches began to fly again. "You two have kitchen duty for a week. And you can start by marching in there and starting something for supper. Jake, this is Mrs. Daniels, and she'll be staying the night."

Jake's and Luke's attention shifted with an almost audible click to Amelia, who tried to smile. They didn't speak—for fear of further enflaming their father, no doubt—but they nodded and then disappeared in opposite directions.

The inside of Fletcher's house, Amelia finally took time to notice, could have been a pleasantly cozy mixture of old chintz furniture and some rough-hewn pieces that might have been antiques. But the place was a mess. A stunning stone fireplace commanded the living room, which was cluttered with schoolbooks, newspapers and assorted shoes, boots, items of male clothing, a saddle that someone was in the process of restitching, and a tumbled pile of firewood that had spilled out of its box and lay in a mess along the wooden floor. Faded white curtains hung in the windows and looked as if they'd been there for a decade.

Some rock-and-roll music thumped from a radio in a distant room upstairs. The piquant scent of spicy cooking hung in the air. The dog, which had followed Fletcher from the plane, made an obedient beeline to a rug by the fireplace, shedding tufts of hair in his wake.

Fletcher threw his hat at a rack of elk antlers, which hung on the wall by the door. The hat missed, but he didn't notice. When he turned back to Amelia and saw her expression, he grinned. "I guess this isn't exactly *Father Knows Best*."

"Your sons seem like . . . nice young men."

"Or The Two Stooges?" Fletcher grinned. "Oh, they're great at first impressions, all right. How about a drink?"

A drink sounded fabulous—preferably a strong martini to calm things down. But Amelia wasn't sure she should accept one. It felt disloyal somehow that she should be comfortable and dry while Zoe was very probably lost in a violent rainstorm on the mountain somewhere.

"Come on," Fletcher said, reading her expression with an uncanny accuracy. "Quit worrying about your kid. Like I said before, she's probably having a ball. You look worn out. You won't do her any good if you have some kind of breakdown, right?"

"I am not having a breakdown."

Fletcher shrugged, still looking amused. "Okay, have it your way. Grab a seat. I'll get you a beer."

He left her alone, heading for the swinging door through which the two boys had slunk just moments earlier. Amelia could hear him berating them in the kitchen. She looked around for the seat he had entreated her to grab, but came to the conclusion that none of the furniture was inviting. She hadn't felt so far from home in years.

In the next minute, Luke Fletcher came thumping down the staircase, looking none the worse for wear, despite his recent altercation. When he spotted Amelia alone in the living room, he looked for an instant as though he might try to tiptoe back up the stairs. But he caught her eye and came politely into the room to talk with her.

"I took your bag upstairs, ma'am."

"Thanks, Luke. I—um—I'm sorry to descend on you so suddenly this way."

"Oh, that's okay," he said. "We have lots of guests. Mostly guys, though—men who come up here to go hunting."

"Of course. Does your father do guide work?"

"A little. Not enough, of course. We're always broke."

"That seems to come with the territory."

He looked at her more closely. "You know my dad very well?"

"No," said Amelia. "I know this country very well, that's all."

"Uh-huh," said Luke, eyeing her with more interest than ever.

Fletcher arrived at that moment, carrying two cans of beer in one hand. "You two getting acquainted?"

"Yeah, Dad," said Luke, already sidling for the kitchen. "She's okay. You could do worse."

Fletcher laughed.

"Am I missing something?" Amelia asked, taking one of the cans from Fletcher's hand.

"Not a thing," he assured her. "How about putting on the old feed bag? The boys had everything ready."

"Really, I don't need any dinner," Amelia began firmly. "I can't intrude—"

"Baloney. You must be starved. Come on. We haven't had a case of food poisoning in months around here."

He dragged her by the arm to the kitchen. It was a long and narrow room with a low ceiling and an oversize trestle table standing at one end. A wrought-iron rack of assorted blackened skillets hung over the stove, and several shelves lined the short wall by the door. They were lined with jars of home-canned fruits and vegetables—a colorful, yet functional display. Amelia wondered what hardworking homemaker had been suckered into cooking for the Fletchers.

Supper was a typical rancher's meal—a pot of chili and some baked potatoes, which Luke flicked out of the oven with a fork and Jake caught them as if he were fielding pop flies, before plunking each one on a plate. They were laughing as Fletcher and Amelia arrived.

Quick as a grizzly snags a salmon, Fletcher intercepted one of the hot potatoes and dropped it on his own plate. He grinned at Amelia. "This is no place for the faint of heart."

"Or the weak of stomach," Amelia observed, eyeing the laden table.

There were no chairs except the one at the head of the table, which Fletcher took himself. The boys found places along the benches on either side of the trestle table, so Amelia took the spot at Fletcher's right hand. As soon as the family was seated, they began to pass plates and platters, all talking at the same time. Amelia tasted the chili, and found that it was fiery hot. After a hasty gulp of beer, she helped herself from a huge bowl of salad and chose a dressing from among the bottles on the table.

It wasn't exactly gracious living, but Amelia was grudgingly impressed by what went on around her. With a houseful of rowdy sons, it would have been easy to allow each boy to fill up his own plate and sit in front of the television or go up to his own room. But it was obvious that Fletcher required his sons to come to the table with clean hands and a willingness to make conversation.

Luke spoke first, describing the events of his day at school—a difficult math quiz, a silly incident in the school cafeteria and how a friend had finally screwed up the courage to ask a girl on a date.

"It was gross, Dad," said Luke, squinching up his face. "I'm never asking a girl to do anything with me."

"Wait till Melinda Hancock starts blinking her eyes at you," taunted Jake. "You'll change your tune."

"Oh, yeah?" Luke snapped. "But I'd never get all googly like you did over Cindy Freemantle."

Fletcher looked up from his chili. "Who's Cindy Freemantle?"

Jake turned bright red and ducked his head over his supper, mumbling, "Nobody, Dad."

Amelia expected Fletcher to demand more information, but he restrained himself and said instead, "Okay, Luke, what else happened to you today?"

Luke finished swallowing his mouthful before speaking. "The guidance counselor stopped me in the hall today. She said she got those scholarship forms she told me about."

Fletcher frowned. "I thought we discussed that issue, Luke."

Luke set his fork down. "Dad, I know I can get one of those scholarships. I just know I can!"

"For how much?" Fletcher asked sharply. "And for how long? What happens if the freebies run out in a year? Then who gets stuck with the bill?"

Amelia listened in silence, noting that she might have missed a great deal of pleasant dinner conversation in her solitary youth, but she had also avoided countless meals spoiled by family arguments.

"Dad," Luke argued earnestly, "the counselor said that the way my grades are, I could get into almost any school in the—"

"Listen, the counselor doesn't know what our bank account looks like." Fletcher jabbed his fork into his baked potato. "I don't trust scholarships."

Amelia couldn't stop herself. "Why not? I got through four years of college plus law school on scholarships."

Luke's eyes popped worshipfully. "You're a lawyer?"

"I work for a firm in New York."

"Wow! And you went to school on scholarship?"

"Most of my expenses were paid for, yes. I had to work to make money for books and whatnot, but—" At last Amelia caught sight of Fletcher's glowering expression. "Of—of course your father knows what's best for you."

"How did you get the scholarship? Where did you go to college? What about law school?"

"Really, I—" Amelia floundered. "I don't mean to butt in—"

"Please continue," Fletcher snapped.

"Yeah," said Luke. "What colleges have good pre-law programs?"

"I'm sure your counselor can tell you things like that. It's not difficult to get in if you're a top student to begin with."

Excited, Luke turned to his father. "Dad, did you hear that? Mrs. Daniels thinks—"

"I heard," Fletcher said shortly.

"My grades are terrific, you said so yourself, and with a couple of good letters of recommendation, I—"

"We'll talk about this later, Luke."

"But, Dad, I can't get into a good law school if I just go to the junior college like Jesse, so—"

"Later," snapped Fletcher.

Amelia felt like squirming. She stole a glance at Luke and found him looking angry, tense and surprisingly pale. His father, oddly enough, looked just the same.

Jake cleared his throat at last. With obvious pride, he announced, "Hey, guys, I got a C on my English paper!"

"That's an improvement," Luke cracked.

Jake turned on him wrathfully. "Hey, school's no big deal for me, understand? I'm going to run this ranch when I get old enough."

Fletcher laughed. "What makes you think it's still going to be here?"

Jake shrugged. "It will. Where's it going to go?"

Luke turned to his father. "I almost forgot. The market called today. They asked us to round up a dozen steer and take 'em into town this weekend."

Fletcher frowned. "They'll have to wait till Monday for the beef, I'm afraid." He nodded. "Okay, after school tomorrow, you guys can get started on that."

Excited, Jake volunteered, "I could cut school tomorrow, Dad, and take care of it myself. Why, you wouldn't have to help or anything—"

"Forget it," Fletcher said. "You're not skipping a single day of school until you graduate, got that?"

"*If* he graduates," said Luke dolefully.

The conversation meandered in several directions after that. Amelia listened and her final impression was one of a tightly knit, totally independent family of individuals. It was clear to her that the Fletchers worked hard together, understood one another and didn't hesitate to express their feelings.

"Chores," Fletcher announced when the meal was demolished.

Amelia knew enough about ranching to stay out of their way for the next hour. Chores around a farm tended to be well-organized and regimented. Fletcher and his sons scattered, Luke staying to wash dishes, the other two donning slickers to run out into the rainy night and complete the numerous tasks required to keep a working ranch financially afloat.

Amelia knew all about chores. She could remember hauling buckets of water for livestock when she was too small to do anything but slide the bucket across the ground. There had been no reward for hard work in her youth, either—not a kind word or even a feeling of contributing something for the family good. She had felt like a slave—one who hadn't been liked very much by the master.

Keeping her memories private, she dried the dishes for Luke, who proved himself to be an expert dishwasher.

"Jake'll put those away," he said, indicating the stack of dry dishes Amelia had left on the table. He whipped off his apron and left it on the counter. "I gotta go see about the dogs."

Fletcher came back into the house around nine-thirty. He stripped off his slicker and Stetson and hung them on a hook by the back door.

"Oh, you found the coffee," he said, seeing Amelia at the sink, rinsing her cup. "Was it drinkable?"

Amelia was struck by the confidence in his movements. He was definitely a man to be reckoned with.

"Not too bad. Want some?"

"Sure. What's one more cup?" He poured himself a mugful from the pot and took a quick, thoughtless gulp. His dark eyes widened immediately. "Wow! This is great coffee."

"I made another pot. What was left could have taken the rust off your airplane."

"What rust?" He grinned and carried his cup to the swinging door. "Come on, I'll show you a bed."

Amelia dried her hands on a towel hanging on the refrigerator door and followed, hurrying to keep up with Fletcher's long strides. He headed up the narrow staircase to the second floor, saying, "The weather's going to dry up by morning, I think. We could get started by eight o'clock, if we're lucky."

" 'We'?" Amelia asked, startled by the possibility of further travel with Fletcher.

"Sure." He cast a glance at her over his shoulder. "You don't plan on making this trip alone, do you? Through that canyon and up the mountain?"

"I'll make better time by myself."

He laughed. "You think so?"

"Face it, Fletcher. I'm in a terrible hurry, and you're not exactly eager to help me."

He turned on the landing. A smile played on his mouth; the glitter of curiosity shone in his eyes. "What gives you that idea?"

"Everything. We could have started before dinner, but you—"

"But I remained calm. If we'd gone rushing off, we'd have accomplished nothing but increasing your next dry-cleaning bill." He tilted his head toward the window. "Listen to that storm. It's a murderous night."

"And my daughter's out there!"

"Better her than you. It'll teach her a lesson."

"I'm not as heartless as you are. Fletcher, I want my daughter back safely!"

He shook his head and headed up the steps again. "Finding your daughter is one thing," he said. "Getting her back is something else."

Stubbornly Amelia followed him up the steps. "Why are you being such a jerk about this? I thought you'd be pleased to get rid of me!"

"Because you're sticking your nose in my family's business, you mean?"

"Luke ought to go to college, you know. He's obviously smart, and he's highly motivated."

"Let me worry about Luke."

"All right, turnabout's fair play. Let *me* worry about Zoe. I'm going by myself tomorrow, Fletcher."

"You'll get lost if you go alone."

"No, I won't!"

He stopped at the first door on the hallway. "The terrain's changed, you know. They're lumbering up at your old man's place, and we've had rock slides. You won't recognize the country."

"I'll manage."

"And eventually I'll have to go looking for your bleached bones? Forget it. I don't have that kind of time to waste." He leaned against the doorjamb, looking down at her.

He had that cocky grin on his face again—the one that lightened his eyes and made Amelia wonder if she'd forgotten to get dressed that morning. Suddenly the air between them was alive with electricity—Fletcher had managed to change the atmosphere with one swift glance down Amelia's body.

Dropping his voice, he said, "I can't let you go alone. What sane man would allow a pretty lady like you to slip through his fingers?"

"Who says you're sane?"

His lazy smile grew. "It's you who's driving me out of my mind, Mrs. Daniels. What is that perfume you're wearing, anyway? It makes my head spin."

Amelia suppressed a groan of frustration. "You have such a way with words sometimes. You don't realize how serious I am about this, Fletcher. My daughter's life is at stake and—"

"No, it's not. You and I both know she's safe. She might be a little uncomfortable, but she's fine."

"I want to be sure of that."

"You will be—tomorrow. In the meantime, why don't you and I get comfortable ourselves?"

"In the meantime," Amelia interrupted before he suggested something distasteful, "all I can think about is Zoe."

"All I can think about is you."

"Fletcher, has anyone ever told you how pushy you can be?"

"Women love it, I'm told. They fall for the tough guy every time." He braced his hand on the doorjamb behind her head, effectively making their conversation more intimate. "Is that true with you, Mrs. Daniels?"

"I'm not falling for anyone—tough or otherwise."

"You're turning down a terrific opportunity."

"I'll survive."

He sighed theatrically and grinned. "Have it your way."

Shouldering the door open, he led Amelia into a small bedroom that was tucked under the eaves at the front of the house. She could hear the rain on the roof above, and when Fletcher snapped on the bedside lamp, she saw a cozy double bed covered with a faded quilt, a bookshelf haphazardly piled with paperbacks and a desk that was cluttered with papers. A closet door hung open, and a flannel shirt had been abandoned on the knob.

Amelia hesitated on the threshold, suddenly sure she was setting foot in Fletcher's own bedroom. She saw that her carryall had been left on the bed.

Fletcher turned to her in the half-light, and must have seen Amelia's expression. He laughed. "Take it easy. I'll sleep downstairs out of respect for your virtue."

"That's not what I was thinking!"

"No?" With a grin, he asked, "Would you rather I stay up here with you and to hell with your virtue?"

Amelia regarded him wryly. "You're a son of a gun, Fletcher. Some strong woman needs to put a lasso around your neck and settle you down a little."

He grinned, standing between her and the bed. "I could go for games like that. Want to try?"

Amelia grasped the front of his shirt and steered him toward the door. "Good night, Fletcher. I appreciate your hospitality, but I'd rather have a hot water bottle to warm my bed—not you. Do you want your toothbrush before you go? Pajamas? No, I bet you sleep in the buff, right?'

He grinned. "It's a tantalizing thought, isn't it?"

"The stuff of nightmares." Amelia pushed him gently into the hallway. "Good night, Fletcher."

When she closed the door in his face, he said from the hallway, "Good night, Amelia."

The sound of his voice lingered in Amelia's ears for a long time. Even when she was undressed and sliding between the time-softened sheets, she could hear the seductive caress of his words and see the easy sexual confidence in his smile.

Amelia told herself she was suffering from having eaten too much of the Fletcher chili. But in her heart she knew it was something else that wreaked havoc with her insides. When was the last time she had allowed herself the pleasure of a man's company? Especially one as attractive as Fletcher?

Perhaps never, she decided. Her friends in New York hadn't the faintest idea what kind of men lived in the West—sexy, physical, quick-witted men. But Fletcher was one of the sexiest Amelia had ever met. He was one of a kind.

She found herself smiling as she drifted off to sleep in his bed.

Three

That night, Fletcher took a blanket and went down to the lumpy sofa in the living room. He didn't sleep, however. Maybe it was too much coffee. Or maybe it was the woman upstairs in his bed. Fletcher found himself imagining all kinds of wonderful adventures in the company of Amelia Daniels.

She was a good-looking woman—very classy with an underlying sensuality he found highly arousing. She had a sense of humor, too—the second thing Fletcher looked for in a woman. He dozed off wondering if she liked to laugh in bed.

In the morning, Fletcher awoke from an erotic dream when Jake came thumping down the staircase, scratching his tousled head and looking startled to find his father on the sofa.

"What happened?" Jake asked, coming to sit on the arm of the couch. "You strike out?"

Fletcher tried to wake up fast. "What? Who?"

Jake waggled his eyebrows. "She's a looker, Dad. I didn't know you still had it in you. I mean, if I'm reaching my sexual peak next year, you must be in sad shape when it comes to a woman like her."

Fletcher glared at his son. "The older the instrument, the sweeter the music, Jake."

"You always have some old saying to fit the moment." Jake laughed. "Funny thing is, Dad, we didn't believe you'd really do this."

Fletcher was rubbing his eyes and figured he hadn't heard correctly. "Huh?"

"When you said you were going to get us out of debt by finding yourself a rich wife, none of us believed you. But man alive, when you walked in the door last night with her—"

"Hold it," said Fletcher, fully awake at last. "That's not what's going on here."

Jake laughed. "Sure looks like it. 'Cept you're not supposed to be sleeping down here on the sofa when the bride is waitin' upstairs. What's the matter, Dad? Have a tiff already? You couldn't keep her happy for twenty-four hours?"

"Shut up for once and listen, will you? I am not marrying Mrs. Daniels. That was a joke, for crying out loud. Do I have to watch every word I say around here?"

"So what's the story here, Dad? You having an affair or something?" Jake looked delighted. "Gee, that's neat!"

Fletcher sighed. Sometimes there was no sense arguing. "Don't you have a school bus to catch?"

Jake grinned. "Not for another hour."

"Well, spend that hour somewhere besides in my sight."

His suggestion wasn't taken seriously, of course. Jake guffawed. Rocking on the arm, he said, "It's nice to know you're normal, Dad. You get grouchy when you're horny, too."

"My God, where did you learn to talk like that?"

"What's to learn? Take my advice, Dad. Don't take too long waiting for the right moment to make out with her, all right? I hear old age has a sudden way of sneaking up on a guy."

With that, Jake headed for the kitchen, swaggering. Fletcher threw a pillow at the boy, but it thumped against the kitchen door a second too late.

Mornings were always hectic, but having a woman in the bathroom made things even worse. Fortunately Fletcher made it into the shower first, and he managed to find some clean clothes in the dryer. Jake and Luke ended up washing in the kitchen sink and prepared to leave for school without brushing their teeth.

"This is gross," said Luke, energetically rubbing his teeth with his index finger. "Can't you go up and chase her out of there, Dad?"

"I'll go!" Jake volunteered, obviously enthusiastic about the prospect of catching Amelia without her clothes. He started up from the breakfast table.

"Forget it," said Fletcher, grabbing Jake's shoulder and pushing him back down into his seat. "One day of bad breath won't kill you."

"When will you get back, Dad?" Luke asked.

"Tomorrow night, if I'm lucky. Sunday if I get held up. In the meantime, you boys will round up some steers and pen them today after school. No funny business, hear? Just get the job done right, or you'll have me to answer to. Got that?"

"Yes, sir," they said in unison.

"And no fighting," he added. When they didn't respond to that admonition, Fletcher considered delivering another of his brotherly-love lectures, but decided they wouldn't listen, anyway. They never did.

"Okay," Fletcher said, dropping his dishes into the sinkful of soapy water. "Go catch a couple of horses for me and Mrs. Daniels before the bus gets here."

Outside, the boys were astonished to find Amelia standing on the paddock fence, already dressed and ready to go in the morning sunlight. Luke came rushing in to tell his father, then dashed upstairs to brush his teeth. Fletcher finished washing the dishes, then with another mug of coffee in hand, he went outside to feast his eyes on his lovely houseguest.

She didn't disappoint. Amelia had on a pair of well-broken-in blue jeans that automatically drew the male eye to her shapely hips and long legs. A blue pullover sweater looked serviceable and matched her eyes with uncanny accuracy. She had brushed out her braid and pulled her hair back into a swinging ponytail—the curly kind that tempted a man's fingers—and it shone like dark gold in the early-morning sunlight. Her boots looked too scuffed to be brand-new. Maybe she wasn't a tenderfoot, after all.

"You remember how to ride a horse?" he asked her when he arrived at the fence where she perched.

"Oh, good, you're here." She climbed down to stand beside him, dusting off the seat of her jeans. "Yes, of course. Good morning."

"'Morning." He hid his smile behind the coffee mug. Even in his dreams last night, he hadn't imagined her looking so delectable as she did standing there in the sunlight. Did she wear lace and satin under those jeans? he wondered.

She refused to meet his gaze, which was an even more intriguing development. Fletcher wondered if Amelia had experienced a few erotic dreams of her own last night.

Innocently Fletcher asked, "Sleep well, Mrs. Daniels?"

"Like a baby," she said promptly—a sure sign that she was lying. "Except for worrying about Zoe, of course. I tossed and turned for a while. I appreciate the loan of your bed, though. It was very—" She stopped herself and started to turn a charming shade of pink. "Well," she began again, "it was quite comfortable. I hope you slept well, too."

"I slept badly, as a matter of fact."

She sent him a steely look, as if guessing another suggestion behind his words. "Too much coffee, perhaps?"

"I don't think that was my problem."

"Maybe you should count sheep. I hear it's relaxing."

"There are better ways to relax in bed, don't you think?"

"I don't know," she said coolly. "I've never had trouble falling asleep."

He laughed. "Maybe I'll pick up a few pointers from you sometime."

She remained composed. "Not this morning. I'd like to get started looking for Zoe."

"Got to get the posse mounted first." He lifted his coffee mug and gestured with it toward the horses. "Which one strikes your fancy?"

Amelia turned her attention to the dozen saddle horses that milled around the paddock. Studying the herd with a critical eye, she said, "I don't know. They're all pretty fit—except that sorrel mare."

Fletcher watched the animal and soon saw the horse was limping, all right. It was very slight, but definitely a limp nevertheless. "Luke," he called, "cut out Dixie and take her up to the barn."

"But, Dad, the school bus—"

"It won't leave without you."

"I'll do it," Jake volunteered, already sliding through the fence.

"You'd make the job last an hour and miss the bus on purpose. Let Luke do it. Take a rope and catch Oberon for me—make it quick. And, slip a bridle on Bianca."

The boys scrambled to obey before the school bus arrived. Amelia said, "Oberon and Bianca?"

"Our Shakespearean period," Fletcher replied. "Luke's idea. Go grab yourself some breakfast. We'll saddle these horses and be ready to go by the time you're finished."

She surprised him by climbing the fence again and throwing one of her slim legs over the top. She dropped lightly into the paddockful of horses. "I'll help," she said, dusting her hands in a businesslike fashion. "I'm not hungry."

She joined the boys in capturing the horses in question, and Fletcher had to admit it looked as though she knew what she was doing. She wasn't afraid of the big animals—not even when a rangy gray gelding bumped her with his shoulder and knocked her into the paddock fence.

"She's got guts," Luke said, passing behind Fletcher with the sorrel mare. "I like her, Dad."

Fletcher didn't reply. He liked her, too. Spunky and determined—and sexy, to boot. He watched Amelia help Jake fasten the buckles on a bridle. She was smiling at the boy in a way that gave Fletcher a pang of jealousy. He wanted a sample of that lovely smile himself. Jake looked completely smitten.

The bus roared into the bottom lane then, horn tooting. Jake shoved Oberon's rope into Fletcher's hand, threw Bianca's reins at Amelia and pelted down the lane toward the bus. Luke darted out from the barn to follow, and they both waved their hats and shouted their goodbyes.

Jake yelled, "This one's okay, Dad! You could keep her a while!"

Diplomatic Jake, Fletcher thought. He waved back, then looped Oberon's reins around a fence rail and moved to help Amelia saddle her horse.

She already had the saddle thrown over Bianca's back and was tying the girth expertly, obviously annoyed by Jake's parting shout. Concentrating fiercely on the job at hand, she said, "I take it I'm not the first woman to stay here at the Ponderosa."

Fletcher balanced his coffee mug on the nearest fence post. "Not exactly," he said. "But you're definitely the best looking in a long time."

The remark did not please her. She finished the knot and turned to him. "Look," she began firmly, "I think we'd better set a few ground rules, Fletcher."

"Ground rules? For what?"

"For you and me. I'm not here for hanky-panky, cowboy. I won't—"

"Hanky-panky?" He laughed. "What the hell is that?"

"It's your brand of suggestive fooling around, and you know exactly what I'm talking about. My daughter is my first priority, and I won't put up with any homespun funny business from you until I find her."

"And after you find her?"

"Dammit, Fletcher, I'm serious!"

"So am I."

"I'm only staying in this wretched country long enough to get Zoe back to civilization."

"Why not stick around awhile and see the sights before you leave? Enjoy the countryside. Sample the local color."

"You're suggesting yourself, I presume?"

"I can be pretty colorful when I want to be."

To prove the point, he reached for her wrist. Amelia was too startled to resist. Her blue eyes popped open wide as Fletcher pulled her close.

When her breasts collided with Fletcher's chest, she said breathlessly, "Wait!"

Fletcher didn't. He slipped his free hand around the back of her neck, tipped her head up and kissed her on the mouth. She squirmed and braced her hands against his chest.

But she didn't push him away—not yet. Her lips tasted warm and sweet, and they parted instinctively. Fletcher kissed her deeply, holding her slender body tightly against his own and marveling how perfectly they fit together—belly to belly, thigh to thigh. He could feel her heart slamming in her chest—and his pulse accelerated to match that swift, excited rhythm. A surge of something hot and arousing washed up inside Fletcher. She was warm and quivering in his arms—quivering with anger, perhaps, but something else, too. Something infinitely more pleasant.

As the school bus roared by, gears grinding, the boys hung out the windows and hooted. The bus driver blew the horn merrily.

Amelia began to fight him then, arching her back and shoving hard. Fletcher had no choice but to release her.

Free again, she backed up and bumped into the fence. Her face was shocked at first, then quickly turned furious. She wiped her mouth with the back of her hand and demanded, "What was that for?"

"I wanted to do it yesterday, but the right moment didn't come up."

"What gives you the right to kiss me?"

"Call it human nature." He crossed his arms over his chest and appraised her. "Having you sleep in my bed last night didn't help matters. I've got an active imagination, Amelia."

Huffy but collecting herself rapidly, she snapped, "I'd have slept on the couch myself if I thought you were going to react like this!"

Shaking his head, Fletcher laughed. "Believe me, you were much safer in my bed. At least there was a lock on the door."

Without thinking, she said, "I didn't lock it."

Fletcher raised his brows. "Why not?"

Shortly she said, "Because I assumed you were a gentleman."

"Is that it? Or could it be that you're feeling the same way I am?"

She swung away from him, went around the tied horse and began to shorten the stirrups. Although Fletcher followed, she refused to meet his eye. Curtly she said, "I'm human, too, that's all."

The bus disappeared, and Amelia finished the stirrup with a yank and came around the horse to take care of the other side. Fletcher stepped out of her way. Watching her fuss with the buckle, he asked, "How long has it been for you?"

She kept her attention on the stirrup. "Are we talking about relationships or sex?"

Fletcher laughed, leaning against the fence. "Maybe there's a difference in New York, but not out here."

"It's been a long time," Amelia said at last. She flipped the stirrup back into place, but kept her face averted. "Having a man around is very awkward with a teenager in the house. I—I'm afraid to date anyone for fear Zoe will hate him. Or maybe she'll like him too much and then I'd feel trapped. My personal life's a mess." She turned toward him, hands on her hips. "How about you?"

The question caught him off guard. "My life's okay."

Her gaze was direct and demanding, and a cold smile played on her mouth. "Tell the truth, cowboy. You're as desperate as I am, maybe more so."

"What makes you think that?"

"The way you look at me. Like I'm a piece of pie and you haven't eaten in a week."

"You're an especially appealing piece of pie, Amelia."

She shook her head, watching his face with those intense blue eyes of hers. "That's not all of it. You're trapped up here with those boys, and despite how much you try to be cool about parenting them, you're as uptight as I am. You can't slip, or they'll catch you, right? How long has it been?"

"Sex, you mean?" Uncomfortably he shrugged. "Not long, really. I get it once in a while."

"Is that true?"

Fletcher hesitated. How had he allowed her to trap him into this conversation? "It's been a while," he admitted.

"Do you date anyone?"

He grinned. "What's a date?"

"Do you have any women friends?"

Fletcher snorted. "I hate that expression, don't you? Friends. As soon as a woman says she wants to be my friend, I know we're sunk." He pulled the saddle off the fence and set it on Oberon's back. "Why do women believe sex and friendship can't go together?"

"Sex complicates things."

"Not for me," Fletcher said firmly. "It makes things easier. When you take your clothes off and trust somebody the way you have to trust them as soon as you climb between the sheets—well, you know where you stand, that's all."

Amelia smiled. "Maybe so."

"It *is* so. Children are complicated. Ranching is complicated. But men and women—that should be simple."

The weight of that remark made Fletcher feel uncomfortable. How had she managed to dig all that philosophy out of him so early in the morning? He hunkered down to grab the trailing girth from beneath Oberon's belly. He had revealed far more than he'd intended.

Amelia held Oberon's head while Fletcher tied the girth. Petting the animal's nose, she said speculatively, "Somehow I didn't picture you having trouble with women."

"I didn't figure you had trouble with men."

"I don't." She smiled sheepishly then. "Mainly because there aren't any men in my life. I have business associates and women friends. No men."

"Because of Zoe?"

"Having a teenager around can be very inhibiting, but that's not all of it. My work is very male dominated. As a woman who wants to get ahead, I have to be careful. It's easier to go without male company than put up with all the hassle."

Fletcher straightened from his task. "Seems to me," he drawled, "we share another mutual problem, Mrs. Daniels."

She smiled wryly. "What problem is that?"

He reached for her wrist again and pulled Amelia closer. "Lack of a sex life."

"I never said—"

He gathered her against his chest again, aware that Amelia wasn't exactly eager, but wasn't pulling away, either. He smiled down at her, enjoying her fearless expression, the droll purse of her lips—those very kissable lips. Softly he said, "Maybe we ought to help each other out?"

She laughed, flattening her hands against his chest once more. "Hold your horses, cowboy!"

He liked the way she touched him—nothing wishy-washy. "It's a logical idea, isn't it? We're alone at last. I find you very attractive, and I can assure you that I'm not an amateur when it comes to tossing hay."

"And you're humble, too, I notice," she countered lightly, remaining in his embrace for a moment—as if she enjoyed the sensation of being in a man's arms again. Her eyes were full of sparkle, her mouth relaxing into a luscious curve. "Humility is one of the first things I look for in a man."

"So how about it?"

Almost reluctantly, she peeled out of his embrace. "I think you know my answer to that proposition. I'm here to find my daughter, remember?"

Fletcher pretended to blow an exasperated sigh. "Kids again? Even when they're not underfoot, they manage to trip me up."

Amelia didn't move for an instant, but remained standing before him, looking up at Fletcher's face with an odd expression on her face. "You surprise me, Fletcher."

"You just noticed how damn handsome I am?"

"No, I just noticed there's actually something of value inside you—something thoughtful behind that cocksure attitude of yours." She allowed another smile. "Unfortunately you keep it well hidden. You're a classic pain in the butt most of the time."

Fletcher grinned. Damn, but he liked this woman!

"Let's get rolling," she said before the moment stretched into something more intimate. "I don't want to stand here all day wondering if we should have gone to bed together last night."

"No need to wonder," Fletcher said lightly. "We definitely should have."

With that, he left her. Inside the house, he made a quick phone call to Mrs. Cobb, a neighbor who cheerfully promised to check on the boys during Fletcher's absence.

"I'll bake them a pumpkin pie," she promised.

"Thanks, Mrs. Cobb."

Then Fletcher collected the food and bedrolls he'd packed earlier, locked the dog in the laundry room so he wouldn't follow and carried everything out into the sunlight again. With care, he lashed all of it onto the pack saddle of a pinto mare he often used for carrying loads. In the saddle room, he found an old Stetson and took it outside to Amelia.

"Try this for size. You'll need it today."

She blew the dust off and brushed the hat against her jeans before slipping it onto her head. Perfect fit. She looked him in the eye and asked, "Who did this belong to?"

"My ex."

"Did she look good in it?"

Fletcher grinned. "It never quite suited her. She was a child of the suburbs, and it showed. On you it looks terrific."

"Don't try to snow me, Fletcher, all right?" She settled the hat more firmly on her head. "Ready to go?"

"Let's get a move on."

He climbed into Oberon's saddle, slipped his aviator sunglasses out of his pocket and put them on. Approvingly he watched as Amelia settled onto Bianca's back as if she'd never been away from horses. She looked good with her slim legs clamped around a saddle. With his heart lifting, Fletcher reined his horse around and pointed him northward.

Amelia felt strangely relieved after kissing Fletcher. The event hadn't scared her. It hadn't caused the sky to break open and fall into pieces around her. It had felt good—wonderful, even. Maybe it was the western sunlight that made things feel different. Or the wide-open spaces. Amelia realized that she felt freer than she had in New York. Less constrained, somehow. It was an exciting sensation.

The sun rose in the sky, casting a sparkle on everything below. Every blade of grass, every rock, every tree gleamed with the moisture left from last-night's rain. The morning air felt cold and clear in Amelia's lungs, lightening her head as she rode behind Fletcher, up the hillside and into the canyon. She could see where the heavy rain had washed out the trail in places.

Between the mountains, a majestic silence reigned. Only the swishing of their horses' legs in the tall grass broke the quiet. The trees had begun to show their autumn colors, and the sight was breathtaking.

The scenery was beautiful, but Amelia tried to steel herself against the magic of the land. She didn't want to be seduced by the beauty of the countryside she had once called home. There were too many bad memories she could associate with the land—the blue-grey mountains rising in the west, the clear streams running with cold, clean water. Everything around her seemed tainted by the man who had wanted to lock her in the hills forever.

As they reached the end of the canyon and began the climb up the northmost crag, Amelia heard a cry from above. Looking up, she saw an eagle plunging down from the clouds—elegant, ferocious. Amelia's throat tightened at the familiar sight. How many times had she watched the eagles and longed to be as free to come and go as they were?

Fletcher had reined his horse by the boulder that marked the trail and waited there, holding the pack horse. He said, "Feel good to be home?"

Amelia urged her horse onward. "Nope," she said shortly.

He watched her go by, clearly bewildered by her reaction. But he didn't ask more questions, and for that Amelia was glad.

She led the way for another few miles. Conscious of Fletcher's curious gaze on her back, she didn't turn around or speak to him, but tried to put his presence out of her mind. Only when he called to her did she pull up her horse.

"Wrong way," he called, gesturing up a washed-out crevice with his hat. "We go up here."

"Sorry," Amelia said when she returned to his side.

"You've been doing pretty well so far," he said. "Ready for a rest? Some lunch, maybe?"

Amelia hesitated, then gave him a rueful and tentative smile. "I'm half-afraid to get down. It's been years since I've been on a horse. I'll be saddle sore."

"Only one way to find out." He looked amused. "Putting it off won't make it go away. C'mon. I've got some sandwiches."

They dismounted, and Fletcher laughed when Amelia's feet touched solid ground and she groaned. Her knees were unbelievably stiff, and her legs felt like jelly. Blood tingled in her veins from hip to toes.

"Go sit down," Fletcher told her, turning uncharacteristically charitable. "I'll loosen that saddle for you."

Just to be contrary, she didn't sit, but hobbled up and down the trail for a few minutes to work the kinks out of her muscles. Fletcher opened his pack and brought out some sandwiches and a couple of cans of beer. He made a picnic on the boulders.

"You want something to eat?" he called. "Or you planning to tough it out?"

She limped over. "What have you for lunch?"

He snapped open a foamy beer and handed her a sandwich to go with it. "Not exactly watercress, but it'll have to do."

Amelia investigated between the slices of white bread and found chunks of cold meat loaf, lettuce and tomato. It tasted heavenly, she decided after one bite. She ate half her portion ravenously until she realized she had forgotten her manners. She finished the rest more delicately.

"Another?" Fletcher asked, raising an eyebrow at the speed with which she devoured her lunch.

She couldn't keep the hopeful note out of her voice. "Are there more?"

Smiling at her eager expression, he reached for his pack again and tossed the food to her. "Fresh air is always good for an appetite."

She unwrapped her second sandwich and eyed Fletcher at the same time. "I assume you're referring to all kinds of appetites, right?"

He laughed. "Like what?"

"You hope I'll say sex."

"I'd be knocked for a loop if you said sex," Fletcher retorted, taking a hearty chomp out of his meat loaf. Mouth full, he said, "You don't strike me as the kind of lady who appreciates pine needles down her jeans."

"I'm not as uptight as you think, Fletcher."

"That's good to hear. You seemed mighty tense yesterday."

"I'm worried about Zoe, of course."

"There's something else, though, right?"

Amelia allowed a nod. "It's the shock of homecoming, I guess. As you may have figured out, I wasn't very happy here."

"Lousy love affair?"

With a smile, she shook her head. "No, it was my father who drove me away. For years I resisted any reason to come back to see him."

He plucked a slice of tomato out of his sandwich and ate it. "Time heals all wounds, so they say."

"Maybe so, but I doubt it in this case." Amelia stared pensively at the panorama spread out before her. The sky seemed endless; the silent mountains rolled to the ocean. Amelia sighed. "When I lived here, I used to feel small and alone. I couldn't wait to see the rest of the world."

"We all spend our childhoods looking for something better, I think."

That remark surprised Amelia. "Did you?"

Fletcher swallowed his last bite and balled up the waxed paper his sandwich had been wrapped in. "That," he said, decisively, getting to his feet, "is a subject for another time."

Amelia was not to be fended off so easily. She nibbled her sandwich some more, asking flat out, "Where are you from, Fletcher?"

He struck a cowboy's stance, playacting a little. "What makes you think I'm not a native of these parts, ma'am?"

"You're not," Amelia said, suddenly sure of herself. "You ride a horse like a natural, but there's something else about you—something that doesn't quite make you a rancher."

"I'm not," said Fletcher, his grin fading. He looked out across the canyon they'd just crossed, watching the land for a moment. Amelia wondered if he was hoping some answers might appear on the landscape. More softly he said, "I want to be a rancher, but I'm not yet."

"What are you, then? Doctor, lawyer or Indian chief?"

He shrugged. "A soldier, I guess."

Amelia watched him for a moment. "If you hadn't mentioned the Purple Hearts, I wouldn't believe you. You seem an unlikely soldier, Fletcher."

"I was a pilot, actually."

"Vietnam?"

He nodded. "My brother and I went together and flew helicopters."

"You have a brother?"

"Sure. Abel. He ended up in Washington—when he's not off adventuring someplace exotic. He works for the Smithsonian, digging up artifacts for the museum. He always was the intellectual type."

"What type are you?"

He gave her a grin. "The type who has a hard time answering to a boss."

Amelia responded with a broad smile. "I'll bet! I have a hard time imagining you as a soldier, you know. Even a pilot. You're a little too goofy."

He exploded in a laugh. "Too *goofy*? I thought I was manly—virile—exciting—"

"You're those things, too, I guess, but—"

"You *guess*?"

"Yes. Mostly you try hard to be funny. It's like you're covering up something, I think."

"Hmm," said Fletcher, a speculative look entering his eyes along with the amusement. "Maybe we're more alike than I first thought."

"What's that supposed to mean?"

"You're hiding a lot, too, lady. You're keyed up about finding Zoe, but you've got a few ghosts to put to rest. This stuff about your old man has you spooked, for one thing. Is there anything else I ought to know?"

"I can't think of anything."

"No spurned lovers hiding in these hills?"

Bemused, Amelia said, "Not a single one, I'm afraid."

"Good. I don't have to worry about any competition in this neighborhood, at least. What about your husband?"

Caught off guard, Amelia asked automatically, "Who?"

"I figure you must have had one once. Do I have to worry about Zoe's father?"

"We're divorced," she replied with a wry smile, amused that Fletcher had circled back to flirting again.

"Great," said Fletcher, climbing to his feet. "You can run, but you can't hide from me, Mrs. Daniels. Need a hand?"

Amelia accepted his help to get herself in a standing position. She winced as a pain shot up her stiff legs. "I don't think there's going to be much running, Fletcher. I'm practically crippled from riding this morning."

"The news gets better and better, doesn't it?"

"Stop that, will you? Help me get on my horse."

With his most devilish grin, Fletcher said, "It'll be a pleasure."

Four

———

Late in the afternoon, Fletcher finally spotted the rooftop of the cabin where Jesse and Zoe had undoubtedly spent their night together. He urged his horse up the path to the building, but soon realized the two teenagers had already departed. No smoke curled from the chimney, and the hoof tracks in the mud around the cabin were many hours old.

Just to be sure, Fletcher called, "Jesse!"

No response. Amelia urged her horse up to the edge of the porch and shouted, "Zoe! Zoe, answer me!"

Silence. Fletcher cursed to himself. There was no telling what the unpredictable Jesse might do just to prove something to the world. He might even take a naïve young city girl and do something very foolish. Carefully Fletcher masked his opinion from Amelia. She'd go off the deep end again if she thought her daughter was in danger from an oversexed teenager.

"Well," said Fletcher, dismounting, "at least we can see they were here last night."

"Can you be sure?"

"Yep. See the tracks? And somebody's poured coffee grounds over there. There will be other signs, I'm sure." He flipped the stirrup over Oberon's saddle and began to untie the girth.

Amelia stayed on her horse. Her voice was sharp. "What are you doing?"

"What's it look like I'm doing? We're stopping for the night."

"Couldn't we make it the rest of the way before dark?"

"Not unless we risk the horses. You know that. They've been going all day."

"But it's only a few more hours—"

"Simmer down. We can't go any farther today, and that's final." He dragged the saddle off Oberon's sweaty back and lugged it onto the porch. With a heave he set it on the railing, and caught Amelia frowning at him. "What's the matter?"

"We're so close to finding them!"

"Not close enough, I'm afraid. It's ten more miles to Brook's place—most of it straight up the mountain. These horses can't make that trip today."

She took off her hat and fanned her face, which was flushed and glowing. Studying the ramshackle cabin, she said, "I really don't want to spend the night here, Fletcher."

"Complaint registered." He thumped back down the steps and reached for Oberon's reins. "Why not look upon this situation as an added bonus? A night of bliss under the stars with me won't cost you an extra cent and you'll still get your kid back in the morning."

"Will we get to my father's place early tomorrow?"

"Unless we sleep late and decide to fool around a little, yes."

She returned his gaze dourly. "We're not going to fool around at all, Fletcher."

"Leastwise not with you looking like that, I must say. Didn't your mama tell you that frowning would make your eyebrows grow? That'd be unattractive."

"I'm not concerned about looking attractive—and certainly not for you."

"Every girl's got to stay in practice." He took hold of Bianca's bridle. "Want some help down from there?"

"No."

But as she moved to climb out of the saddle, Amelia gave a squeaking kind of moan, and her legs gave out completely. Fletcher caught her before she hit the ground by grabbing her around the waist. She lost her balance and ended up in his arms, leaning heavily against him, breathing in pained gasps.

"My God," she said, panting. "I don't think I can walk!"

Fletcher supported her. "You're going to be one sore little cowgirl by morning, aren't you?"

Amelia's face twisted with anguish. "You should have dropped me by parachute, Fletcher. A couple of broken legs couldn't be as bad as this!"

"Legs as nice as yours should never be broken. Let me help." He scooped her off her feet and swung Amelia into his arms.

She clutched his shirt for support. "Fletcher, put me down this instant!"

"Are you kidding? I've been waiting all day for a chance like this."

"I'm not an invalid!"

"Shut up and enjoy the ride." He carried her up the steps of the porch, blowing a mouthful of her ponytail out of his way. "I never carried a woman over the threshold before."

She tilted her head to look up at him curiously. "What about your ex?"

"She walked on her own two legs. She wasn't much of a romantic."

Amelia smiled despite her obvious pain. "Are you a romantic, Fletcher?"

For a moment he was seized by the urge to kiss her then and there and make her forget completely about being saddle sore. But Fletcher settled for bestowing upon her one of his sexiest grins. "You'll have to wait and see."

She seemed unaffected by the grin, but rather raised one doubting eyebrow and suppressed a smile. Looping her arms around his neck in a ladylike fashion, Amelia held on as Fletcher strode across the porch. She felt wonderful in his arms—soft curves, slender limbs and fragrant hair.

She said, "I have a theory about you, Fletcher."

"Oh-oh."

"I bet you rescue lost puppies and sniffle over sad movies."

"Me? Hell, I never sniffle. An occasional beer-induced belch, maybe, but—"

"I guess I'll have to wait and see about that, too, won't I?" She cast a single bemused look up at him, causing Fletcher to stumble. For the first time all day, he noticed the sprinkling of delicate freckles that were scattered along the pert bridge of her nose.

Manfully, he restrained the urge to press kisses on those adorable freckles and instead kicked open the cabin door with a flourish.

"Welcome to the presidential suite at the Hotel Fletcher, Mrs. Daniels. What do you think?"

Amelia obviously thought the place was a dump, and Fletcher had to agree. A bare cabin with a tottering old table, one broken chair, a kerosene lamp and a heap of firewood piled near the fireplace. Standing in the center of the drafty room, Fletcher heard a mouse scuttle through a hole in the outer wall.

"Elegant," Amelia said, eyeing the hole where the mouse had dashed. "When can we call for room service?"

"The management will be sending up champagne any minute, I'm sure."

"Champagne? For you?"

"Well, we'll have to settle for a six-pack of something less high falutin', but the effect's the same, I'm sure. Is it safe to put you down?"

"I think so."

With extreme care, Fletcher set Amelia on the table for lack of a better spot. "How's that? Feel better?"

She stretched her legs cautiously. "I'll be all right, I think. Just give me a couple of minutes to limber up. And maybe you could bring my bag in here? I've got some aspirin in it."

"Coming right up. Then I'll take care of the horses, and we'll have some supper."

She nodded. "Let me know what I can do to help."

"Help?" He crowed with laughter and turned to leave. "You city girls only know about microwaves and Chinese takeout. We're going to have a real wilderness meal, lady, and *I'm* going to cook."

"Heaven help us."

"You wait," he promised, already out the door. "You're gonna love it."

It wasn't exactly a gourmet meal, but Amelia did love it—at least, she appeared to. She dug into the hot dogs and beans cooked over an open fire with gusto, as the flames snapped and flickered cheerfully while the darkness fell around them. The smell of steaming coffee filled the air, mingling with the scents of wood smoke and hot food. The evening breeze turned pleasantly chilly. Munching their picnic, Fletcher and Amelia sat side by side on the porch steps and watched the stars come out in the inky-blue sky.

"You're a useful kind of guy, Fletcher," she said as she licked the last of the catsup off her fingers. "Do you wash windows, too?"

"That's what children are for, right?"

Amelia sat back, bracing her elbows on the steps behind her. "I guess you're not exactly the best housekeeper I've ever met."

"You didn't like my house?"

"It could use a good cleaning. Otherwise it's charming."

He shrugged, mouth full of hot dog. "Unfortunately I've got champagne tastes and a beer budget. We're relatively comfortable—that's what counts."

"From hearing you talk to Luke, you're relatively broke."

"The college thing? Yeah, money's part of it. Mostly I don't want him to leave yet. He's too young. His teachers bumped him ahead a year, so he's academically ready, but I don't want him to have the same experience Jesse did—leaving home before he's ready. Hell, he's only fifteen."

"A pretty grown-up fifteen," Amelia remarked. "It wouldn't hurt him to develop a few champagne tastes of his own, you know."

Fletcher studied Amelia's earnest face and decided he didn't want to think about being a father for a while. He said, "Maybe it's time to call room service for some champagne for us."

Amelia laughed as he got to his feet. "I wish we could just telephone." She sighed, gazing up at the sky. "I'd love some champagne on a night like this."

"Your wish is my command." Fletcher climbed into the porch, then hunkered down and removed a rock from the porch stonework. He reached into the secret chamber until his whole arm disappeared. He grinned as his hand made contact with the object inside. "Aha. Still here."

He withdrew his arm and came up with a dusty bottle. Triumphantly he blew the dust off. "I hid this a long time ago and never thought to look for it until now. It's a wonder the boys didn't find it and guzzle the whole bottle ages ago."

Amelia took a peek at the label. "A California wine?"

"Some of the best. Not champagne, but just as good in my book. An old 'Nam buddy of mine started a vineyard in the Sonoma country a few years back. This was one of his first vintages. I had a bottle once before, and it's good stuff—unless the weather's ruined it. Want to try?"

"I'm game."

Fletcher used his pocket knife to pull the cork from the bottle. He had packed two collapsible metal cups, into which he poured the wine. The drink sparkled in the starlight, hissing with a natural effervescence that was music in the otherwise silent evening air.

Presenting the first cup to Amelia, Fletcher said, "Not exactly leaded crystal, but who cares? Know any good toasts?"

"Like 'here's to your health' or something?"

He poured his own cup full, put the bottle aside and turned toward her again. "Or something. What shall we drink to?"

Amelia wondered what he was up to. To be safe, she suggested, "Long life?"

"Boring, Amelia." He tipped his cup against hers, the back of his hand brushing Amelia's fingers in a way that could have been accidental—except that he continued the touch for another moment. Suddenly he seemed very close, but Amelia couldn't draw back. Fletcher's dark, liquid eyes were full of firelight, and he gazed at Amelia with such intensity that she felt herself tingle inside with expectation.

His voice dropped to a husky murmur. "Let's drink to serendipity—the good fortune that's brought us together on a night as beautiful as this."

Amelia drank as if hypnotized by his steady gaze. The wine slid sweetly down her throat, reaching her stomach and suddenly spreading from there through her entire bloodstream with a kind of magical glow.

"Good?" Fletcher asked softly, watching her eyes as the wine took effect.

"Very good." Her voice was suddenly so weak that she was whispering. The wine tasted fruity, yet dry on her tongue. Its sweetness came later—a kind of afterglow that was delicious. "I hope your friend is making a fortune by now."

Still clasping his cup, Fletcher rubbed his rough knuckles on her fingers again, then extended the caress to her wrist and up Amelia's goose-bumply arm. He said, "There are other things more important than fortunes, Amelia."

"Like what?"

"Beauty, for one thing. You're a very beautiful woman, you know. You probably hear that all the time."

"Not very often."

"More's the pity. I think you're the sexiest lady I've laid eyes on in a long time."

Lightly Amelia said, "I think we're getting onto shaky ground, Fletcher. Either that, or the wine's gone to your head."

He smiled. "I do feel a little shaky, I admit. You're doing something to me."

"Not on purpose, I assure you."

"What about you?"

"What about me?"

Just as softly as before, he said, "You can't deny that you have felt something between us."

Amelia took another gulp of wine, hoping to steady her nerves. It didn't work. She felt weaker and weaker by the moment. Her voice even trembled. "Sure, I'll admit you're an attractive man."

She could hear the grin in his voice. "You think so?"

"I'd be blind not to notice—well, I mean, you're hard to ignore."

"You've been doing a pretty good imitation of ignoring me all day."

"I have not! I—I—" She caught sight of his expression and crumbled even further. The truth slipped out. "I'm just trying to be cautious, that's all."

He slid a few inches closer on the porch steps. "What fun is there in being cautious, Amelia?"

"Maybe none, but . . ."

"But what? What's the sense in keeping yourself tied up in knots when you could let go on a night like this and enjoy yourself a little—a lot, in fact?"

He leaned closer, and Amelia's sensitive nose caught the rugged scent of him—mostly wood smoke and wine combined with a tougher fragrance that was Fletcher's own. It was a tempting smell—manly and enticing. If he ever set foot in Manhattan, Fletcher would be mobbed like a rock star. He had that sexy, arrogant quality that made so many women swoon.

Amelia found herself smiling. "That's what I like about you, Fletcher—not a moment of self doubt."

"Oh, I've got a lot of doubts, Mrs. Daniels. One is that I doubt I can stop myself from kissing you right now."

"Fletcher—"

"You want me to?" He used one knuckle to lift her chin a fraction of an inch.

Amelia felt a tiny part of her body start to betray her—a warm, twisting reaction deep beneath her stomach. "Fletcher, I—"

"I want to kiss you very badly. I've wanted to all day." He caressed her throat then, drawing little whorling patterns with his knuckle first, then his thumb. "Haven't you felt the same way?"

"Maybe," whispered Amelia, her voice breaking nervously.

"A long kiss," Fletcher said, finding her throat at the spot where her heart beat closest to the skin. He played his forefinger over the spot. "Nothing quick like this morning. I want a long, slow kiss from you, Amelia."

"We should exercise some self control, Fletcher."

"Is that what you really want?"

Amelia closed her eyes to revel more completely in his caress. "You're seducing me, Fletcher."

"And you're crumbling, Amelia."

She was, indeed. Fletcher's mouth brushed hers very softly at first—tantalizing her. Amelia turned her head to catch his lips more firmly, but Fletcher avoided that maneuver and instead swooped closer once more to softly brush one tiny kiss after another along her cheek, her temple, the bridge of her nose. It was a technique Amelia hadn't guessed Fletcher would use, yet here it was, making mincemeat of her composure. Amelia quaked inside, unable to open her eyes for the delicious sensations he aroused in her.

He whispered her name. Then Amelia heard him set his cup down on the porch—it made a quiet *clink* in the cool night air. In the next moment, Fletcher took her face between his calloused hands, slipping his fingers into the strands of her hair that tumbled around her face. She opened her eyes and found his dark gaze drinking in her face as if memorizing every detail. There was a hint of laughter in his eyes, but mostly Amelia saw a hungry intensity that shook her to the core of her soul.

He brushed his lips across her cheek, murmuring, "Such sexy freckles. I wonder if you have them all over?"

"You'll never find out, will you?"

He laughed deep in his throat, a sound that caused Amelia to quiver inside. She closed her eyes as he lowered his head and captured her lips with his own. It was a warm, long, thorough kiss meant to shatter her resolve completely. And it worked. Slowly Amelia's body began to ache and throb and finally start to burn inside, and his tongue found its way inside her mouth and began to tease hers with slow, sensual strokes. Her hands crept around his neck of their own volition and tangled in the thickness of his dark hair.

Taking that as a signal to press further, Fletcher pulled her closer by wrapping one strong arm around her waist and drawing Amelia inescapably against his hard frame.

She couldn't resist. He felt deliciously strong, wonderfully powerful, and his mouth played erotic games with Amelia's lips and tongue. She didn't have the will or the strength to pull away.

His other hand smoothed down her back, then found its way to the front of her sweater. Amelia held her breath—half her brain shrieking a warning; the other half cried out for his touch. He must have heard her wanton half, because in the next second Fletcher's warm hand slid up under her breast and cupped it. She gave a languorous sigh as he caressed her while sucking gently on her lower lip at the same time. Without thinking, she arched against his body.

"Sexy lady," he whispered.

Weak with excitement, Amelia said, "God, Fletcher, what are you doing to me?"

"I'm about to start taking off your clothes," he muttered. "You'd better stop me now, if you're going to. I'm fast reaching the point of no return."

She saw in his face that he was just as affected as she was. His eyes were full of fire, and his breath came in quick bursts. She didn't have to look any further to know he was as aroused as a man could get. Taking her lack of response for an affirmative answer, he moved to pull her sweater up and bent his head to find her breast with his mouth.

"Wait," she said, bracing her hands against Fletcher's chest and holding him off. Even the idea of his mouth roving freely on her bare flesh sent Amelia trembling again. But she stopped him reluctantly.

He lifted his head and looked at her with a hungry expression. "Yes?"

Amelia took a deep breath. "Fletcher," she began, voice quaking, "you're making this very difficult. Under different circumstances..."

"Like what?" he asked, coming closer again to nuzzle her earlobe. "If we knew each other a few hours longer?"

"That would help!" She laughed, her voice trembling in the night air. "But even then, even if I could forget about Zoe and relax, it wouldn't be right."

"Oh, it would be very right, Mrs. Daniels."

She smiled. "Quick and easy, is that it? Simple sex with no strings attached."

"Simple sex?" He laughed. "No way, lady. The more complicated the better, if you ask me. Why, we could—"

"That's not what I meant, and you know it."

"Yes," he said using his finger to slip a wisp of her hair behind her ear. "I know what you meant. But I'm not listening."

"You have to listen, Fletcher. I want you to listen. I can't make love with you."

"Can't or won't?"

"Won't. Not tonight—and probably not ever. I'm not sticking around after I find Zoe. I'm taking her back to New York as fast as I can. We're not going to see each other again."

"So we should be making a connection now. We've got a chance to do something meaningful—"

"Meaningful?" Amelia laughed. "Sometimes when I'm around you, Fletcher, I feel like I better put on a pair of waders! You have more lines than the average lounge lizard from New Jersey! What you want is something I'm not going to give—a single night's entertainment that's going to make me feel cheap and foolish in the morning."

"I think," he said, tantalizing her with another whispery kiss along her hairline, "I can make you feel worn out and satisfied in the morning."

She pulled out of his embrace determinedly. "Don't try to muscle me, Fletcher. I don't like being manipulated."

"I call it seduction."

"It's the same thing."

He wasn't going to be a jerk, thank God. Fletcher released her gently reluctantly. "Okay." He sighed, making his regret plain. "I gave it my best shot."

"It was a pretty good one, too," Amelia admitted. "But I intend to get a good night's sleep so my head will be clear tomorrow."

"Lady," said Fletcher as he stood up and put out his hand to help Amelia to her feet, "you're going to get a terrible night's sleep. You're going to dream about me all night long, and by morning you'll be a bundle of hormone-crazed nerves."

Amelia didn't believe him—not at first. But when she rolled up in the sleeping bag he provided and lay down on the cabin floor by the fire, she began to wonder if he wasn't right. Fletcher came in eventually and lay down beside her, moving quietly to avoid waking her.

Amelia pretended to sleep, but peeked at his profile in the flickering light. When she was sure he wasn't watching, she studied the appealing break in his nose, the subtle curve to his lips and thought about the way he'd kissed her on the steps outside. She still felt aroused. It would be easy to roll into his arms and find out exactly how cowboys made love.

She hugged herself tight and tried to control the urging from inside her own body. Softly she said, "Good night, Fletcher."

He turned his head toward her, and she thought she could see the sparkle in his eyes. He said, "Sweet dreams, Amelia."

Five

___

In the morning, Amelia awoke to a dream in which Fletcher's arms were tight around her. When her head cleared, she realized his arms *were* tight around her and his nose was buried in her hair. He was breathing rhythmically—clearly sound asleep in his own sleeping bag, which meant that *she* had been the one to ease across the floor and snuggle up. Amelia's own body had traitorously surrendered to some internal need during the night. She was curled instinctively against the curve of his warm frame. Their sleeping bags had become hopelessly twisted together.

Blushing furiously, Amelia carefully disengaged herself from the weight of Fletcher's arm. She held her breath and tried to sit up without waking him. No luck.

Fletcher blew a long sigh and rolled onto his back, blinking hard to wake up. "Damn." His voice rumbled. "Morning already?"

"I'm afraid so. And it's awfully cold." She pushed her hair off her face and watched him gingerly stretch and start to groan as his tendons creaked and his bones sounded like popcorn in a hot skillet. Amelia frowned. "Are you all right, Fletcher?"

He waved her concerns away. "It'll take a few minutes, that's all. My kids say I'm getting old. It's times like this I think maybe they're right."

"You don't act old, Fletcher."

He grinned at her. "That's the nicest thing you've said so far, Mrs. Daniels. You getting sweet on me?"

Amelia laughed. "Heaven forbid." She folded her legs Indian-style and tried to rake her hair into place. "It's just that I've never been around a man who was so determinedly young at heart."

"Anything else is counterproductive." He sat up on one elbow with a groan, then began to openly admire her appearance. He looked mighty appealing himself at that moment—handsomely tousled and approachably sleepy eyed. In a voice half an octave lower than usual, he said, "You could take a few things less seriously yourself, y'know."

Amelia stretched her arms overhead. "Don't start on me first thing in the morning, okay? Give me a chance to get my defenses in place."

"If I didn't need a toothbrush pretty badly this morning, I'd take advantage of those weakened defenses of yours." His eyes roved down her figure.

"Saved by morning mouth." Amelia climbed stiffly to her feet. "My God, I may never get on a horse again. Where's my bag? I think I'd better take some more aspirin."

Watching her stumble around the cold cabin in sock feet, looking for her bag, Fletcher stayed in his relaxed position on the floor and suddenly asked, "When you're not sleeping in your clothes, what do you wear to bed?"

"Fletcher, you're incorrigible."

"I need to know, Amelia. It'll make me happy since you rejected me last night. Have a heart. What do you sleep in? Something French and lacy? An old sweatshirt? Nothing, perhaps?"

"No sense perpetuating a false impression. I favor flannel, I'm afraid, Fletcher." She located her carryall and dug inside for the aspirin bottle. "I'm not exactly a sex symbol."

"That depends on your point of view," Fletcher replied, looking decidedly pleased with her answer. As if renewed, he threw off his sleeping bag and crawled to a sitting position.

Amelia swallowed her aspirin without benefit of water. She was that desperate. Her entire body ached abominably. Judging by the groans of pain that came from Fletcher as he experimented with each of his limbs, he wasn't much better off. But they both managed to get their boots on, clean up the gear inside the cabin and go out onto the porch to greet the morning together.

The sunrise was magnificent—a ballet of pastel colors radiating from the sun as it edged over the horizon. A soft mist lay in the hollows below their mountainside retreat, and the trees whispered with the first hint of gentle morning breeze. As the rays of sunlight crept along the treetops, the rainbow of autumn foliage grew more intense with every passing minute. Though nothing seemed to move, the land was alive with color, sound and scent.

"Makes you glad to be alive, doesn't it?" Fletcher asked, standing just behind Amelia as she drank in the landscape.

She wasn't surprised when he wrapped his arms around her and pulled her back against himself. It felt good, in fact—the right way to absorb the panorama. Amelia leaned against him for a moment, watching the mist as it began to waft and disperse.

Half to herself, Amelia said, "I'd forgotten how beautiful the sunrise could be out here."

"I thought you hated everything about this country."

"I thought so, too. I guess it's just the people in it that I can't stand."

"Hey!"

"Not you," said Amelia hastily. She turned in his arms, anxious to snatch back her thoughtless remark. "I didn't mean that, I'm sorry. I have a lot of bad memories stored up—memories that colored the way my whole life turned out."

"You didn't turn out so bad."

She laughed stiffly. "That's what you think. My relationship with my father has never been resolved. Inside, I'm still a mess fifteen years after I left."

"You look neat and tidy to me."

Amelia shook her head. "My father is a cold man. I hated that quality in him, yet it's probably the one way I resemble him most. Why, I can't even communicate with my own daughter!"

"There's still time to fix that."

Amelia looked up into Fletcher's face. It was an honest face—usually filled with good humor but occasionally radiating a thoughtful brand of intelligence. The compassion she read in his dark eyes gave her a measure of hope. It seemed strange to be accepting such support from a stranger.

But Fletcher didn't seem like a stranger anymore, either, she admitted to herself. In a very short time,

Amelia felt as if she knew him well, indeed. And oddly enough, she wanted to know more.

His hands moved gently on her shoulders, and he asked, "Want some advice from a guy who's a classic pain in the butt?"

She smiled. "Sure."

"If I don't like the way something's going, Amelia, I find a way to change it."

Amelia shook her head. "I can't change things between my father and me. I've made a life for myself somewhere else—that's what's important. I have friends and a great job. I don't need him."

"Maybe he needs you."

"That's a laugh!"

"You might be surprised," said Fletcher. "Some guys have a hard time communicating what they need. Sometimes it just takes one person to make a move and everything's better."

Amelia noted the gleam that entered his eyes, and she felt the subtle change in his embrace. He drew her closer until Amelia's body was aligned snugly with his own.

She smiled. "Are you about to make a move, Fletcher?"

"I've been making moves since we met," he said, dipping his head closer yet. "In case you haven't noticed."

She fended off the kiss before it started, laughing as she pushed on his broad chest. "What about that toothbrush, Fletcher? I thought you were going to be chivalrous about this."

He gave up reluctantly. "All right, I'll give you a break this time. But pretty soon, lady, you're going to run out of excuses."

He kindly pumped water from the rusty pump several yards from the porch and allowed Amelia some privacy with the bucket while he took care of the horses. For breakfast, he conjured up some stale but edible biscuits and a couple of apples, which they ate while packing the gear. After that, they made sure the fires were cold before they swung into their saddles and headed up the mountain.

Within an hour, Amelia's euphoria quickly faded.

What she saw on Tucker's Mountain took her breath away.

"That's the lumber company," Fletcher explained when they crested a ridge and reined their horses to stare at the devastation that spread in every direction. The trees had been hacked out of the forest, and what was left was a muddy wallow full of tire tracks and bulldozed ground. The hillside had caved in with rock slides.

"They've been cutting timber up here for the past six months. I hear Brook tried to hold them off, but he couldn't manage by himself."

"The mountain is ruined!"

Amelia couldn't believe the destruction. A bomb blast might have caused the sight she saw that morning.

"They say they'll reforest the area," Fletcher said. "But you and I both know they can't replace the variety of natural species found on this mountain. It will take centuries for the forest to come back the way it was."

"And then someone else will come and cut the trees all over again!"

"No doubt. But that's the way it goes. Would you rather have people starve and go homeless, or waste a few trees?"

"Don't try to be objective about this, Fletcher. You're as upset by this as I am." She had seen the determined clench in his jaw as he stared out at the landscape.

"I am," he agreed. "But what can I do? Brook Tucker made the decision to sell off this timber long ago. Now that he's seen what can happen, he wants to terminate his contract with the company. You're a lawyer. You know how that goes. The process will end up in court eventually, but while the legal process plods along, the lumber company goes about business as usual—destroying timber as fast as possible. Brook might get satisfaction in the end, but the land will be spoiled long before."

"This is tragic," Amelia said softly. Her childhood playground had been violated, and Amelia felt as if her own body had been scarred, too. A sick feeling welled up inside her.

Fletcher watched her for a moment. "You're not so hard-hearted about this country after all, are you?"

"Anyone who saw this mess would feel the way I do." Amelia realized she had started to cry, and she dashed the tears from her face. "I'm very sad. And outraged at the same time. How could my father let this happen?"

Fletcher shrugged. "People make mistakes."

Angry, Amelia urged her horse forward. "Let's go, Fletcher. For once, I actually have something to say to my father."

Behind her, he said, "I'll bet it's not going to be how much you missed him."

They rode together for three more hours. Fletcher had to lead the way, because Amelia couldn't recognize anything without the trees. Picking their way cautiously through the rubble, they spoke very little.

At last they crossed into the untouched forest again and stopped briefly to rest the horses and have a snack.

"How much longer, Fletcher?"

"An hour, maybe. You still in a rush?"

"Of course!"

"Have you thought about what you're going to say to Zoe?"

Amelia had spent the morning fuming about her father. "Not really. I assume something will occur to me on the spot."

Fletcher tightened the girth on his saddle again, saying, "Maybe you'd better plan something just in case. It's the spontaneous stuff that can get you into trouble."

"You giving me parenting advice, Fletcher? You, of all people?"

He turned and smiled at her. "The way I look at it, we're in this together, Mrs. Daniels. It's us against them."

"I hope it won't turn into a battle."

"It's already gotten to that stage, hasn't it?"

He swung atop his horse and set off again. Amelia followed close behind, mulling over his suggestion. But try as she might, she couldn't think of a thing to say to Zoe—at least, nothing that would convince her daughter to come home again.

There wasn't time to come up with anything, anyway. Fletcher had miscalculated the distance. In twenty minutes, Amelia found herself riding into the basin where her father's buildings stood.

It was a jolt to see the place again. And this time, through the eyes of an adult, she was shocked by how primitive the settlement looked. Brook Tucker lived in a rustic log cabin set on a foundation of solid rock that rose out of the mountain. Four more smaller cabins—usually rented to visiting hunters, fishermen or tourists—stretched down the mountainside beneath the trees.

But it was the main cabin that drew Amelia's attention. The porch was still crooked. The chimney leaned precariously to the north just as it had fifteen years ago. The stone steps were cracked and broken—unrepaired after all these years. Half a dozen scrawny horses—not the ones Amelia remembered from her youth, but amazingly similar—stared balefully out through the rails of their makeshift corral.

A badly constructed stone barbecue still dominated the clearing, for Brook often used it to cook for his visitors. Amelia remembered the countless nights she fell asleep to the sound of male laughter outside the cabin as strangers ate and drank with her jovial father. How many times had she wished he could be half as jovial with his own child?

She sat on her horse as the memories flooded into her mind. She couldn't stop them—the way the bears used to invade the clearing, drawn by the smell of food. How frightened she'd been listening to them fight among themselves and hurl their huge bodies against the cabin door to gain entrance. How many tourists had passed through her life? Hundreds of strangers had shaken her hand, tweaked her cheek, tugged her pigtails. At first she'd been friendly with them, but as she grew older, Amelia had felt their attitudes change. She had known instinctively to keep her distance as she'd become a woman. Her father wouldn't have come to her rescue if she'd needed him, she was sure. She'd been afraid he might bawl her out for not pleasing the customers.

How many times had she accompanied her father on his once-monthly trips to town for supplies? And every time they returned to the cabin, she'd felt almost physically sick at the thought of another month of loneliness. No wonder she had run to the nation's biggest city! Amelia had surrounded herself with as many people as possible—hoping to make the human connections she longed for in her youth.

Fletcher got down from his horse and automatically reached for Bianca's bridle, too. His voice snapped Amelia out of her daze. "Hello!" he called, his rich voice filling the clearing. "Anybody home? Hello!"

Amelia's voice shook as she cried, "Zoe! Where are you?"

As if by magic, the door of the cabin swung open, and Zoe herself stepped out into the sunlight. At the sight of her daughter, Amelia felt her heart almost stop beating entirely. For an instant she could only rejoice that Zoe was alive and well. She looked like a mountain fairy—her flaxen hair a halo around her scrubbed, perfect face.

Fletcher must have heard her sharp intake of breath. He touched Amelia's leg and said, "Take it easy, Mom. She looks fine to me."

Amelia quickly dismounted, leaving her horse in Fletcher's care. She hurried up the path, wanting only to hold Zoe hard—to touch her and make sure everything was fine.

But Zoe's first words were "What are you doing here?"

Amelia faltered on the steps. "I've come looking for you, of course." Her voice choked with tears. "Oh, Zoe!"

She flung her arms around her daughter and hugged. The teenager stood rigidly in Amelia's embrace, then halfheartedly put her arms on her mother's back.

She said, "You didn't have to come, Mom. I can take care of myself."

Amelia released her, but held on to Zoe's hands. Her own eyes were swimming with tears so she could hardly distinguish Zoe's features—her upturned nose, her wide-spaced blue eyes, the tiny chip in her front tooth from a swimming accident when she was seven. "Of course I had to come! Darling, you scared me to death!"

Zoe's eyes narrowed. "Don't start, okay?"

"Don't—? Zoe, do you realize what you've done? When I got your note, I was frightened out of my wits! I thought maybe you were kidnapped or—"

"I told you what I was doing. I wasn't kidnapped." Zoe carefully avoided making eye contact. She looked at the clearing where Fletcher stood holding horses. "Who's that? The pilot?"

"He's a friend now. He helped me find you. I—"

"I wasn't lost, y'know."

"You were lost to me, young lady." Amelia heard her own voice harden. "You had no business terrifying me the way you did."

"What about the way you treated me?"

Amelia blinked. "You're equating sending my daughter to the best school in the country with running away? See here, Zoe—"

"Look, Mom, there's no reason for you to be here if we're just going to have the same argument."

"This isn't an argument. It's a question of right and wrong."

"It *is* an argument, and the usual one. That's why I left, y'know. I couldn't stand it one more time."

"Zoe—"

Fletcher interrupted then. He had tied the reins around the nearest tree stump and come up onto the steps. He said, "Hello, Zoe. Nice to see you're safe and sound."

"Fletcher—" Amelia began, exasperated.

He said, "Take it easy, Amelia. You're not handling this conversation very well, anyway. How you doing, Zoe?"

Amelia huffed. "Now listen, Fletcher—"

"Hi again," said Zoe shyly. Her wide eyes traveled up his tall frame, measuring the configuration of his chest and shoulders. "I guess you're Jesse's dad."

"Right." Fletcher shook her hand. "But don't hold that against me. You got a ride, I see."

She nodded. "Another pilot took me. He was—well, I didn't like him much."

"He hurt you?"

"*What?*" Amelia cried.

"He didn't hurt me," Zoe said, not surprised by Fletcher's question. "He was a jerk, though. I managed him okay."

Fletcher nodded. "Good for you. And Jesse?"

Zoe looked blank. "What about him?"

Amelia jumped in, unable to stop herself. "Zoe, this is exactly what I was afraid of. There are strange men everywhere who would take advantage of a nice girl like you. You're darn lucky to have come this far without something truly terrible happening—"

"Nothing terrible happened, Mom. I'm fine. I got here by myself, and I like it."

"*Like* it?" Amelia laughed shortly. "That won't last, I guarantee. I'm taking you home."

"No, you're not."

"Now look—"

"I mean it, Mom." Zoe stood her ground, shoulders hunched and face tight. "I'm staying here. Granddad says I can."

Amelia's heart turned to stone. "He does, does he?"

"Yes, I can stay as long as I like."

"Forget it. You're coming home."

"Er—" Fletcher started, trying to make peace.

"I am not," Zoe snapped, voice rising. "I'm staying here."

"I'm your mother! If I choose to take you to live in Timbuktu, young lady, you'll go!"

"You'll have to tie me up first!"

"If I have to, I will!"

"I hate you!" Zoe screamed. "I hate you. I hate you!"

She bolted away and ran down the steps, stumbling blindly on the cracked stones.

"Zoe!" Amelia shouted. "Come back here this instant!"

Fletcher grabbed Amelia's arm to prevent her from giving chase. He hung on grimly, even when Amelia fought to get loose. "Hold it," he commanded.

"Let me go, Fletcher!"

"Just take a minute to think, will you?"

"Dammit, let go!"

"Amelia, stop!" he ordered. "This isn't the way to handle anything. Will you simmer down? Use your brains, lady!"

His command finally penetrated Amelia's anguish. She stopped struggling and watched Zoe disappear into the forest. Sadly, she said, "Oh, Fletcher, I blew it, didn't I?"

"You didn't handle it real well," Fletcher agreed.

He used his thumb to rub her cheek, and Amelia realized that she had been weeping. She skimmed the rest of the tears from her face with her own hands. "Damn," she said. "Everything I said was wrong."

"Heat of the moment," Fletcher commiserated.

"I meant to say I love her."

He cradled her easily in his arms. "Would you have come all this way if you didn't?"

"She needed to hear it, though. Sometimes actions aren't enough."

"You'll get another chance." Fletcher stroked Amelia's jaw. "She'll be back. There's no place to run from here, unless she plans on walking the whole way to Canada."

"Maybe I should go after her."

He held her tighter to prevent Amelia from running after Zoe. "Give her time to calm down. You'll both be ready to discuss this situation in an hour or two."

Amelia sighed and glanced up at his face. "Thanks, Fletcher."

He laughed. "For what?"

"For barging in before I ruined things completely."

"I'm good at barging," he agreed, dark eyes full of amusement.

They heard a noise close by and turned together, startled. Standing in the open doorway was a young man—tall, dark haired and devastatingly handsome. He was about eighteen, Amelia guessed, and in many ways the spitting image of his father. Even the way his soft jeans slouched on his hips was exactly the way Fletcher's did. Jesse's expression was sullen, and his black eyes reflected pure hostility.

"Uh," said Fletcher, clearing his throat, "Mrs. Daniels, this is my son Jesse."

Jesse said, "I bet you don't call her 'Mrs. Daniels' when you're alone."

Fletcher's voice grew tense. "Say hello to the nice lady, Jesse."

"Hello," Jesse said to her, but his gaze was locked on his father.

"Hello," Amelia replied faintly. The air was crackling with tension, and she decided she'd rather not see Fletcher in action as a parent. "I think I'll take a walk to clear my head. Will you excuse me?"

Under his breath Fletcher said to her, "Chicken."

"You have things to discuss. I'll be back in a while."

She left them glaring at each other and hurried on foot up the hillside through the trees. She chose a direction that was opposite from where Zoe had disappeared, and as she walked, she realized she hadn't chosen the path by accident.

The narrow path twisted sharply up through the rocks. It was well used, Amelia noticed. Someone walked the trail regularly. As she retraced the steps she had taken a thousand times, she wondered if someone else had taken up her vigil after she had left her father's house.

At the top of the hill, overlooking the valley where the sparkling creek ran among the rocks, Amelia slowed her steps. Ahead, the sunlight danced between the branches of the trees, casting a pattern of light on the gravestone.

By habit, Amelia plucked a wildflower from the ground and carried it to her mother's grave. She crouched on her heels and put the flower at the base of the carved stone.

Mary Martha Tucker

The name had been carved in fancy script. There were no dates, no further information. Only Amelia and her father ever laid eyes on the stone, and they knew everything that needed to be known about the life and death of Mary Tucker. No other words were needed.

Amelia stayed on the quiet hilltop for a long time. She saw that the grave had been neatly kept in her absence. The grass was trimmed, the flowers in place. That task had been hers while she lived on Tucker's Mountain. She had taken it upon herself at the age of twelve—on a summer's night two days after her mother's death. Every night thereafter, Amelia had walked up the path and tended the grave. She had talked, too. Though one-sided, those conversations had kept Amelia's sanity all those years. She was certain of that.

Her mother had made Amelia's early years on Tucker's Mountain magical. A teacher by profession, she had educated Amelia at home, supervising book work at the kitchen table every morning and taking long walks in the forest every afternoon. They discussed literature, geography and mathematics, but the subjects hadn't been as important to Amelia as the spiritual bonding with nature that her mother encouraged. Under her mother's tutelage, Amelia had learned how the mountain breathed and grew, slept every winter and regenerated itself each spring. She had learned about life and love on those long afternoon walks.

After her mother died, Amelia continued those walks, ending each day by stopping by the graveside to talk. She had poured out her anger, her fear, her loneliness. Talking to her mother had been a way of verbalizing her feelings, of getting her pent-up emotions out in the open. But it hadn't provided any real answers. Amelia had found those in her own heart.

She remembered how bitterly she resented being sent to town to live in the house of a minister so she could attend public school. She lay in her cramped bedroom every afternoon, counting the days until the weekend, when she could pour out her soul to her mother again. That had been the worst time—four long years of having no home at all, before she'd finally run away to the East.

Amelia did not speak as she crouched by the stone that afternoon. She crouched by the marker, however, and brushed the lichen from the stone.

Suddenly sensing the presence of another person, Amelia stood and turned quickly, then found she couldn't move.

Brook Tucker—white haired now and seeming a great deal smaller than Amelia remembered—stared back at her from the break in the trees. He wore a faded pair of overalls, a whitened flannel shirt, the same clothing he'd favored for decades. In the crook of his arm he carried his gun. The stock was broken open, of course. His shoulders were stooped, but other than that he hadn't changed much at all. A grizzled beard disguised the lower half of his face. And in his blue eyes burned the same open dislike as before.

He spoke in a voice that rasped. "My God," he said. "You look more like her than ever."

Six

___

Enlightenment dawned at that moment. Amelia found her voice. "Is that why you disliked me so much? Because I look like my mother?"

Brook put his head down, and for an instant Amelia thought he was going to leave. Without saying a word, he might turn and go—that was his style. But he didn't leave this time, and Amelia wondered if she'd seen a moment of pain cross his features. It disappeared quickly, though, and he came up the path slowly.

Amelia saw that he had a limp now. It was very slight, but a sign of his age nevertheless.

He stopped on the other side of the grave and stood for a moment, gazing down at the smooth grass. Amelia realized that she was trembling like a child.

At last he said, "She was a beautiful woman, your mother."

Amelia couldn't speak. Not yet. Too many years of resentment prevented her.

Brook shot a look at her from under his bushy white brows. "You're a lot like her."

Amelia swallowed. "Is that a compliment?"

He jerked his head, clearly not intending to answer the question. Gazing down at the headstone, he said, "Your little girl's pretty, too."

"Thank you."

"Who's her daddy?"

"A man I met in New York."

"Where is he now?"

Amelia shrugged. "He was a college professor. He accepted a job in Texas, I think. We're divorced."

Brook frowned. "You took a marriage vow. You ought to have kept it."

"I was looking for a family," she said more calmly than she felt. "I wanted it as quickly as I could get it. I guess I should have been more careful."

He let her meaning slide by unremarked upon. "You raising that girl by yourself?"

"Her name is Zoe, not 'that girl.' Yes, I am raising her by myself."

"Not doing a very good job of it, I hear."

Amelia clenched her teeth. Anger vibrated inside her. "I'm doing the best I know how. I didn't have a very good teacher, you see."

He shot her another look—a glare, this time. "I never claimed I was much of a parent."

"You weren't a parent at all. You were a caretaker, and that's it."

Brook's face began to flush. Gruffly he said, "After your mother passed on, I should have sent you someplace, I suppose? To an orphanage, maybe? Would that have made you happy?"

She laughed shortly. "Do you think you can scare me with that old line now? At first I was scared to death you might actually send me away. Then I started wishing you really would. That's when you stopped threatening me with the possibility."

Watching her, he asked, "Not much different from your own girl, are you? Running away, I mean."

"Zoe didn't run away. She just—she wanted to see this place for herself, that's all. I'm sure she was as shocked as I was to see the mess."

Brook's laser-blue gaze challenged hers. "Saw the lumbering on the mountain, did you?"

"Yes, we did. Why did you sell the rights?"

He shrugged. "They were mine to sell."

"It looks terrible."

"I know. Done a hell of a lot of damage to the streams, too. Fishing is bad. No hunters want to come up this year, either."

"So you're broke despite the lumber contract?"

"I'll make ends meet," he snapped. "Besides, I'm going to stop those bastards before they make things worse."

"How?"

"With this gun, if I have to."

"Don't be a fool," Amelia said sharply. "You'll just end up in jail and the land will still be ruined."

He grinned coldly through his beard. "Maybe I have a lawyer in the family who'd get me out of jail."

"Forget it," said Amelia. "I might like you better if I knew you were behind bars."

Brook eyed her for a long moment and finally said, "Maybe you're not so much like your mama as I thought."

"No," said Amelia, "she was only responsible for half my genes."

Brook began to smile. He brushed his weathered hand through his beard. "You've grown up, haven't you? You didn't use to fight back."

"I've learned a lot since I left this place. I've come to get Zoe to spare her some of those hard lessons you gave me. She's coming back to the city for a good education and a chance to be around people."

"You think you can convince her to leave?"

"I'm going to try," said Amelia. "And you had better not get in my way, understand? I don't want you interfering in my family's business!"

She left him after that, striding across the hilltop and plunging into the forest again. Only when Amelia was sure she was out of his sight did she break down. Her emotions got the best of her. She leaned against a pine and wept bitterly into her hands.

Eventually she pulled herself together and returned to the cabin.

The horses had been unsaddled and turned loose in the corral. There was nobody in sight except for Fletcher, who was sitting on the porch steps. As Amelia got closer, she realized he was nursing a badly bruised eye.

"My God, what happened to you?"

He managed to look amused and annoyed at the same time. "Jesse and I had a few words."

"Good heavens, Fletcher, you had a *fist fight*!"

Fletcher had to admit it was an embarrassing state of affairs. No one had been more surprised than he when he'd been knocked to the ground and abandoned as Jesse stormed off into the woods. His pride was stinging. "Well, *he* threw the first punch. He caught me off guard."

Amelia's eyes widened even further. "You didn't hit him back, did you? Your own son?"

In a growl he said, "I should have, the son of a—" Then Fletcher stopped, realizing he was about to cast aspersion on himself. "How bad does it look?"

Amelia took his head in her hands none too gently and tilted it to get a better look. "Let me see."

"Ow!"

"Big baby. Hold still."

It soon became obvious from her expression that Fletcher was going to be sporting a black eye during the next few days.

Meekly he asked, "How bad is it?"

"There's some ice inside, I'm sure," she said. "It might help." She released his head, absently adjusting a lock of his dark hair—a gesture Fletcher didn't miss.

She glared at him, fists on her hips. "Fletcher, I'm surprised at you. After all that talk about keeping a cool head and planning what you're going to say, you ended up fighting with Jesse?"

"Like I said, he did the fighting." Fletcher dabbed gingerly at his swelling eye. "Anyway, sometimes it's good to just stand still and take a punch."

"What in the world did you accomplish by that?"

Fletcher shrugged. "I let the kid get angry so he'd get over it sooner."

"Has that technique worked before?"

He grinned sheepishly. "To tell the truth, this was the first time I've used it. I'll let you know how it works out."

Amelia began to smile and finally to laugh, shaking her head. "We're a pair, aren't we?"

She looked lovely standing there in the sunlight with a sad smile on her face and her eyes still glassy from crying. Fletcher's heart contracted in his chest, and he caught her hand. "Maybe when this is all over we ought to write a book."

"*Good Parenting in Ten Thousand Easy Steps*?"

"*Kill or Be Killed, Raising Adolescents*?"

"I like that one better. Honestly, Fletcher, neither one of us is doing very well at the moment, are we?"

"Things will get better," he promised. "How can they get worse?"

"Good point."

With the smile still lingering, she met his gaze directly, and something electric jumped between them. Fletcher felt it instantly, and he could see Amelia's expression change, too. Sometime in the past twenty-four hours, they had become intimate friends. And oddly enough, they were both comfortable with that.

"How about some ice for that eye?" she asked. When he nodded, she pulled Fletcher to his feet. Together they went inside the cabin.

Brook Tucker's home was as ramshackle and cluttered on the inside as it was outside. The main room was mostly decorated with hunting trophies, fishing gear and gun racks. Brook's bunk near the fireplace was rumpled with discarded clothing, outdated sporting magazines and a portable radio. On the floor near the fireplace Fletcher recognized Jesse's sleeping bag. He caught a glimpse of a sleeping loft overhead and hoped that Zoe was bunking up there by herself. The situation would become explosive if Jesse and Zoe had started a relationship that involved sleeping together.

"Well, thank heavens," Amelia said, crossing the cramped room to a spanking-new refrigerator that hummed in one corner. "At least he replaced that old icebox."

She opened the freezer and dug around for some ice cubes. She filled a threadbare kitchen towel with them.

"Sit down," she told Fletcher.

He did as he was commanded, sitting on one of the benches at the wobbly kitchen table. When Amelia approached with her makeshift ice bag, he said, "Careful, please. I bruise easily."

"I'll bet. There, feel better?"

"It hurts like hell, as a matter of fact."

Amelia held the ice against his eye, slipping the fingers of her other hand through his hair to hold him. "How's that?"

"It'll get numb, soon, I hope." She was standing very close—close enough to touch. But Fletcher restrained himself. She was feeling fragile, he could see. In a while he said, "I have a hard time imagining you growing up in a place like this, Mrs. Daniels."

"Me, too."

"And Brook Tucker for a father?" He shook his head. "That's really hard to swallow."

"He and I are more alike than you think."

Fletcher glanced up at her. "I can see where you get your stubborn streak, I guess. How'd it go with him just now? You talked with him?"

"We never talk. We argue," said Amelia.

"You came back looking like you'd just tangled with a ghost."

"I did, in a way."

"Make any progress with him?"

"Look, Fletcher," she said. "Let's get one thing straight. I didn't come here to make peace with my father. I came for Zoe."

"You could kill two birds with one stone."

She was adamant. "I have no desire to change things between my father and myself. We live totally separate lives now."

Fletcher blew a sigh. "You sure know how to hold a grudge."

"It's not a grudge. It's just the way things are."

"Okay," said Fletcher. "Just remind me never to get on your bad side."

They were interrupted at that time by the arrival of everyone else. Perhaps Brook had gone looking for the teenagers, because he herded them up onto the porch, and the three of them burst into the cabin together. Amelia nearly dropped the ice bag into Fletcher's lap.

"Zoe," she began, taking a step toward her daughter.

Zoe froze in her tracks.

Brook held up both hands to call for order before any shouting broke out. "See here," he said. "We're not going to have any more squabbling until I've had my supper. Understand? Fletcher? You got a problem with that?"

"Squabbling is bad for digestion," Fletcher said promptly.

"Exactly," said Brook, glaring at his daughter. "So we're going to eat a meal in peace. But first we've got to cook it, and I'll need everybody's help."

He organized the work force quickly after that, sending a sullen Jesse to fetch firewood, Zoe to set the table and Amelia to make biscuits.

"You remember how to do that?" he asked her belligerently.

"I've done it a million times," she shot back. "How could I forget even if I wanted to?"

He grunted and left her to the task.

"Fletcher," he said at last, "I need your help with the beer."

"Sure," Fletcher said amiably. "What can I do?"

"Help me drink it," Brook said. "You look as if you could use one."

So Fletcher accompanied Brook Tucker out to his famed barbecue and helped him grill venison steaks while drinking Canadian beer out of bottles.

Fletcher had met Brook a few times, of course. Who could live in the vicinity of Tucker's Mountain and not know the man? They had been introduced in a hardware store in Missoula once and had met a second time in a bar along the highway. Once, Fletcher had been rounding up cattle and found Brook fishing along one of the creeks that ran between their properties. At that time, they'd enjoyed a leisurely conversation about trout before going back to their own tasks.

Fletcher couldn't say that he liked Brook especially. The old man was ornery and stubborn and not entirely civil, but he was a modern-day mountain man, Fletcher supposed, and mountain men weren't supposed to have drawing-room manners.

Nor were they supposed to have lovely daughters that Fletcher was seriously considering seducing. How would Brook Tucker react if he knew the lascivious plans that lurked in Fletcher's mind at that very moment? Was he the kind of father who pulled out his gun at any hint of impropriety? Or was Amelia correct in assuming Brook didn't give a damn what happened to her?

Brook startled Fletcher by broaching the subject himself as the barbecue smoke billowed around them, effectively screening the two men from the rest of the group.

"Fletcher," Brook said as he poured bottled sauce onto the sizzling meat, "what's going on between you and my girl?"

"Uh," said Fletcher, caught off guard. "What do you mean?"

Brook glared at him from under bushy white eyebrows. "You know what I mean. A woman doesn't look at a man the way she looks at you unless there's something bubbling."

"I can assure you," Fletcher began, with the vision of a shotgun wedding dancing in his head, "that we've only met a few days ago and—"

"Doesn't matter how long you've known the girl." Then, using language usually reserved for discussions that took place among men who'd been drinking for hours around a campfire, he asked if Fletcher and Amelia had gotten to know each other in the biblical sense.

"No," Fletcher said quickly, thankful he could tell the truth.

"Not for lack of trying on your part, I hope?"

Fletcher cleared his throat and wondered if he should be planning a quick getaway. "She's an attractive woman—"

"I suppose so. She's got her ugly side, too. What she needs is some hard use from a man like yourself."

"Well, sir," Fletcher said, "I don't think that's true. My bet is she's had enough hard use. She's looking for something else."

Brook's glare intensified. "What's she looking for?"

Fletcher shrugged. "What all of us are looking for, I guess. Love. Trust."

Brook snorted. "Those things are worthless, son."

"You think so?"

"I know so. And I'll tell you why. They're worthless because they don't last. Things change. People die. There's no sense getting your guts twisted up over a pretty face, Fletcher. You'll only end up with a bellyache."

He slathered more barbecue sauce over the steaks, using fierce concentration to get the job done right. The smoke surged around his heavily lined face, and Fletcher thought he'd never such such a perfect picture of a lonely man in his life.

A voice interrupted from several yards away. "Granddad!"

Zoe appeared, carrying a cracked platter with both hands. She smiled at the sight of her grandfather wreathed in smoke and coughing from the heat. "Granddad, you're going to need a facial after all this work."

"A what?" Brook demanded, bewildered.

"A facial." Zoe tugged his beard playfully. "You take some avocado and make a puree, and put it on your face for a while. It's really good. We'll try it, okay?"

"Who the hell buys avocados?"

Zoe laughed. "Everybody does, Granddad! But if you don't have any, we'll just have to fake it."

"Fake it?"

"Sure. We'll use cucumbers or something."

"Girl, if you think I'm going to do a damn fool thing like smear smashed vegetables on my face, you'd better think twice!"

"I'm going to mix it myself," Zoe countered, not the least bit afraid of her grandfather's pique. "You'll love it—wait and see. Now, here are some vegetables that Mom says you're supposed to cook with the steak."

Brook eyed the slices of onion, peppers and tomato that Amelia had carefully skewered on narrow sticks. "I'm not supposed to put these on my skin, huh?"

Zoe laughed. "No, silly! These are for supper. Now cook them before Mom gets mad."

"Your mom is always mad," Brook grumbled, but he took the platter from Zoe's hands and went to work dropping the skewers onto the grill.

Dinner wasn't as uncomfortable as Fletcher feared it might be. At least, not at first.

Working like a team that had long ago established a rhythm, Amelia and Brook got the food on the table at precisely the same moment. Brook turned on the radio so they could listen to a sportscast while they ate, and everyone found places along the benches of an outdoor table that Zoe had set with mismatched cutlery and a colorful collection of plates. She had placed a jar full of wildflowers in the middle of the table. As he took a seat beside Amelia, Fletcher noticed that the teenager had even folded the paper napkins into little crowns at each place.

"What nonsense is this?" Brook demanded, plucking his napkin from the middle of his plate.

"Put it in your lap, Granddad," Zoe chided sweetly, teasing him. "It's supposed to catch your dribbles."

He sent her a glower and made a show of shoving the corner of the napkin into his shirt collar. Zoe giggled at the biblike effect.

When the food was passed around, Brook turned to Fletcher and said, "I remember you once said you had a passel of children, Fletcher."

"Yes, sir. Three boys."

Brook aimed his fork at Jesse, who was silently picking at his food. "This your oldest?"

"Yes."

"Where's the rest of them?"

"At home. They have school and chores to do."

"They alone?"

Fletcher nodded. "They're old enough. And a neighbor looks in at least once a day."

Jesse made a noise in his throat.

Brook said, "You say something, boy?"

"No, sir."

Brook directed the next barrage of questions at Jesse. "Why aren't you in school, son?"

"I graduated already," Jesse replied, carefully avoiding his father's gaze. "I finished high school in June."

"You have a job?"

"No, sir."

"Why not? You look healthy enough."

"I was—I went to college for a couple of weeks."

"A couple of weeks? What kind of education can you get in a couple of weeks?"

"I was just—I decided it wasn't the place for me, sir, that's all."

"Uh-huh," said Brook, spearing a bite of venison. "So what are you going to do with yourself now?"

Fletcher said, "He's going back to finish the semester, that's what he's going to do."

Jesse glared openly across the table. "I am not."

Fletcher suddenly didn't feel like eating. He leaned forward, both elbows on the table. "Look, Jess, I paid for that semester because you wanted to go so damn badly—"

"I'll pay you back!"

"With what?"

Jesse was trembling with anger. "I'll work it off, if I have to."

"Here, here," Brook cut in, banging his knife on the table. "We're not going to squabble at this table."

Fletcher took a deep breath to steady himself. Zoe looked embarrassed, and Amelia didn't move a muscle. Jesse looked furious, and Fletcher wasn't feeling so hot himself. "All right, I won't squabble," he said. "I only want to make one more point."

Jesse's jaw jutted. "You gonna tell me what I can and can't do?"

"No," said Fletcher. "I guess you're too old to be ordered around anymore. I just want you to understand that I love you."

Jesse blinked. Amelia reached over and put her hand on Fletcher's arm. Her touch felt good and gave Fletcher the courage to keep talking.

"I want what's best for you," he continued. "Sitting on a horse and daydreaming isn't the way to spend your life. I know because I did it for a lot of years before I pulled myself together."

"After the war," said Jesse softly.

"Yes, but that's no excuse. It was wasted time that I wish like hell I could take back. There are things I could have worked on—things with your mother and your brothers that would be different today if I'd gotten back on track sooner. I don't want you to throw away some perfectly good years the way I did just because you don't know what you want to do with yourself."

Jesse looked down at his plate. "I need some time, Dad." His voice quavered. "I need some time away from you."

Fletcher tried not to wince. He hated the thought of parting with any of the boys, but Jesse was the one, Fletcher realized, that he would have the hardest time letting go of. Jesse was special—his first child, the one so like Fletcher in many ways. Jesse was reckless and full of fun, but also the most introspective, the most sensitive to what went on around him. He'd been a difficult child to raise, yet the one Fletcher felt the closest kinship with. It was going to hurt badly when Jesse left.

"I don't want to come home and work on the ranch," Jesse said. "I have to get out on my own. I want to get a job for a while so I can pay back the tuition money."

"Where are you going to get a job?"

Jesse shrugged. "Missoula, maybe. I could pump gas there. Or I thought I'd try to get a job working cattle in Texas."

"Texas is too far away," Fletcher objected at once. But when Amelia jiggled his arm, he said slowly, "Well, let's not make that choice right away, all right? Give it some thought before you go chasing off half-cocked."

"Okay," said Jesse, looking warily at Fletcher, as if he expected his father to snatch back the words at any minute. But Fletcher didn't.

"Well, that's settled," Brook Tucker declared with obvious relief. "How about another beer, Fletcher?"

"Sure."

"I'll get it," Zoe volunteered, jumping to her feet. She hurried into the cabin, returning very soon with two bottles. Fletcher noticed she had taken the time to open the one meant for her grandfather, and she brought him a cigar, too. Brook took it without acknowledging her small kindness and set about digging some matches from his pocket.

Zoe poked Jesse's shoulder. "I'm going to do the dishes," she said. "Come help."

Jesse looked peeved. "Who died and made you boss?"

"Come on, jerk. Haven't you heard? You guys lost the sexual revolution."

Brook guffawed. "Go on," he urged the boy. "You might start a new revolution."

Jesse climbed to his feet and looked appalled as Zoe piled his arms full of dirty plates. He followed her grudgingly into the cabin.

Beside Fletcher, Amelia stood up, too. "I think I'll go referee."

"Nonsense," said Brook, slugging back a hearty swallow of beer. "It'll be good for those two youngsters to talk awhile. They've got more in common than you think. Why don't you find yourself a place to sleep before nightfall?"

She looked at him steadily. "Is the first cabin still a home for skunks?"

"Not anymore, but you couldn't guess by the smell."

"All right," she said. "Then I'll take number three. Fletcher can have the last one. Will you send Zoe down when she's finished?"

Brook shook his head. "Zoe's already settled here in this cabin."

"But—" Amelia stopped herself from protesting. For an instant, she looked as if she might argue further, but she refrained. At last she said, "All right. Good night."

"Good night," said Brook, blowing cigar smoke.

Fletcher watched Amelia leave the clearing, and wondered how soon he could follow her.

Seven

Amelia built a fire in the fireplace of the third cabin, but forgot to open the flue until the room began to fill with smoke. While the cabin cleared, she went outside to sit in the dark on the porch. In a while, Fletcher came strolling past with his sleeping bag over his shoulder. He looked sexier than any mortal man had a right to look. He stopped on the path and took a moment to study the picture Amelia made sitting there with her chin in her hands and her knees tucked tight against her chest.

He said, "You look lonesome."

She forced herself to sound lighthearted. "I needed some solitude. Any more fireworks?"

He sauntered a few steps closer. "Not up at your father's place, if that's what you mean." Fletcher's smile began to gleam in the half-light. "Are you planning some of your own? And if so, am I invited?"

Amelia felt a smile tugging at her lips. His easy slouch seemed even more casual than before, and the bruise around his eye gave him a more devilish appearance than ever. "Fletcher," she said softly, "I think you've had a few beers too many."

"Maybe just enough," he countered, arriving at the bottom of the steps and bracing one boot on the first stair. He leaned down until their faces were nearly touching. "You look lovely in the moonlight, Amelia."

Amelia reached up and tweaked his nose. "Is there an Irishman in your ancestry, Fletcher? Because you're full of blarney this evening. There isn't any moonlight yet."

"Hmm. Well, if there was, you'd still look great. Honest."

He kissed her to make his point—a brief yet powerful kiss on the mouth that let Amelia know he wasn't drunk at all. It was Amelia herself who felt dizzy all of a sudden. The warmth radiating from Fletcher's tall frame, the heat of his kiss, the quickening of her own pulse made her head reel.

She sat back, unable to meet his eyes until she collected herself again. With her head bent, Amelia said, "You were honest with Jesse at dinner tonight, Fletcher. I was impressed."

She could hear the grin in his voice. "You must be more easily impressed than I thought."

Amelia shook her head, taking a peak at his face. "It took courage to tell him that you loved him. It was a very nice moment."

"Like you said, I guess sometimes people need to hear the words."

"I understand how he must feel. You cast an awfully big shadow, Mr. Ross Fletcher. It must be tough for a boy like Jesse to grow up under a man like you."

"A man like me?" Fletcher leaned a little closer again, still smiling. "What do you mean?"

Amelia tried to resist the sex appeal that he so effortlessly exuded. Like everything else about Fletcher, it was impossible to ignore. His supreme self-confidence—whether it concerned women or children or horses or anything he put his hand to—was written in the way he moved, the way he spoke, the way he thought.

Amelia said, "You're a very strong man, Fletcher. Strong willed, strong personality, strong beliefs. You're used to being the boss. Believe me, I know what I'm talking about."

Fletcher took a strand of Amelia's hair in his fingers and twirled it gently. "Do I scare you, Mrs. Daniels?"

"A little, yes."

He put out one hand and ran one fingertip down the curve of her cheek. The gesture made Amelia shiver with an anticipation too powerful to quell. Fletcher said, "You touched me at the table tonight, remember? It wasn't much, I know, but I haven't been able to think about much of anything since then. Your father and I talked for an hour up there, and I can't remember a single thing he said to me."

Amelia's voice quivered slightly. "He probably talked about fish."

"Maybe so. But I wasn't thinking about fish. I was thinking about you."

With a deep breath, Amelia said, "I've been thinking about you, too, Fletcher."

"Good things, I hope."

"Dangerous things, I'm afraid." Reluctant but determined, she caught his hand to prevent further caresses.

Fletcher studied her tight expression. "I'm not a dangerous guy, Amelia."

"Yes, you are. And together, you and I could be very dangerous, indeed."

"But you're tempted, anyway."

He leaned down and brushed his lips across her temple, then down to her earlobe. She closed her eyes instinctively—to better enjoy the sensations he coaxed from her nerve endings. Oh, yes, she was tempted all right. The sandpapery stubble on his face felt wonderful. Involuntarily she released his hand. At once Fletcher's fingertips played games on her throat, even sliding under the collar of her shirt a few inches to locate her heartbeat.

He murmured, "I want to make love, Amelia."

"We shouldn't."

"We're alone," he argued gently. "Everybody else is going to stay in your father's cabin tonight. We can do whatever we want. And I want you very badly. It's the same for you, isn't it?"

"Maybe so," Amelia said on a gulp. "But it's not right."

"It's very right."

"But it's—it's—"

"Yes?"

She struggled with her self-control—longing but afraid, amused but anxious. "It's—"

"Come on, Amelia, what is it?"

"It's irresistible," she finished on a sigh. "Oh, Fletcher."

He laughed and dropped his sleeping bag with a thud. Slipping his fingers into her hair, he cupped Amelia's face so that even if she wanted to, she couldn't escape his kiss.

His mouth tasted warm and sweet and infinitely delicious to Amelia. His teeth nibbled erotically on her lower lip, sending hot messages deep into her belly. When his tongue rolled hers, she heard a quiet moan, and realized two heartbeats later that it was her own. Her hands had found the solid contours of his chest, and against her palm, she could feel how raggedly Fletcher breathed.

She broke the kiss first, then knew at once it wasn't over—not for either of them. She wrapped her arms around his shoulders and pulled herself to a standing position. Their bodies melted together. He felt wonderfully warm, deliciously strong. With Amelia standing on a step higher than he was, she could look him squarely in the eyes. His were smiling wickedly, full of undisguised passion. Then Fletcher wound both arms around her and pulled Amelia tight against his lean and sexy frame. She could feel every muscle and sinew and knew exactly how badly he wanted her.

Nose to nose with her, he murmured, "You're shivering, Amelia."

"Take me inside. I've built a fire already."

"I know," he whispered, finding her mouth once more. He kissed her long and thoroughly then, while Amelia's hands began to explore his body as if under their own command. Kissing him back, she learned every angle of his frame, every button on his clothing. He was on fire, all right. The heat of passion burned on his skin. She unfastened a few buttons on his shirt, and Fletcher groaned when her hands played rhythmically on his ribs.

At last she trailed her fingertips down his jeans and encountered the taut muscle of his thigh. Fletcher didn't breathe for an instant as Amelia found the proof of his desire for her. Then he moved against her hand. "God, lady," he said, his voice rasping. "Do you know what you're doing to me?"

Before she could answer, he gripped her hard and kissed her deeply, plunging his tongue into her mouth as if he could plumb the depths of her soul. His hands grasped her buttocks, lifting her inescapably against his loins.

When she could speak, Amelia gasped, ''Make love with me, Fletcher.''

Without another word, he snatched her off her feet. Amelia wrapped her trembling arms around his shoulders and held tight as he carried her up the steps and through the open door of the rustic cabin. He shut the door with his knee and spun around to look for the bed. There were four rough bunks along the walls opposite the fireplace, and Amelia had already spread her sleeping bag out on the largest of the four. Fletcher headed for it, striding across the plank floor.

''You sure about this?'' he asked as he set her on her feet again.

She leaned against him, weak and breathless. The only fact Amelia was sure about was that going to bed with Fletcher was a big mistake. It wasn't that they might never see each other again—though that possibility weighed heavily on her conscience. Something far riskier gave Amelia pause.

She was in danger of falling in love with him.

Ross Fletcher of Nowhere, Montana, wasn't in the habit of making commitments to women—his divorce and infrequent love life attested to that. He wanted good sex, fun sex, and then he'd be finished. He was probably capable of making love and saying, 'So long forever,' in the morning. He'd say it with a smile, of course. But he'd say it nevertheless.

Amelia knew she was going to get her heart broken. But she couldn't stop herself.

She said, ''We'd better make this a night to remember, Fletcher. That's all I have to say.''

He was already unfastening the buttons at the top of her pullover, laughing under his breath. "Tonight's going to be *the* night to remember, Amelia. For the rest of your life."

Obviously trying very hard to take his time, he kissed her face, her lips, her throat—at the same time peeling off her clothes with great care. Amelia's shirt came off easily, then her bra. Shyly she moved her arms to cover herself, but Fletcher held her wrists.

"Let me look," he coaxed, his gaze filled with firelight.

"I'm nervous."

"I don't believe that." He loosened her hair, spreading it around her bare shoulders. "God, I could look at you all night."

"Fletcher, I— Listen, I haven't been very good at sex."

Casting a doubting look down at her, he caressed her throat, then found one bare breast with his warm hand. The nipple bloomed against his palm, causing Fletcher to smile. "Look how your body reacts to me, Amelia. Don't tell me you're not good at this."

"I'm not. I'm inhibited and repressed and—"

"You just had the wrong partner."

He bent his head slowly and brushed her breasts with his lips—first one erect nipple, then the other. Amelia shuddered with pleasure, reaching up to support his strong nape as he blew tiny kisses on her sensitive flesh. As she held his dark head against her breast, she watched his face as the firelight flickered over his features. He looked hungry as an animal driven to seek sustenance—an expression that excited her. As she watched, Fletcher closed his eyes and took one aching nipple in his mouth.

She nearly fainted. It felt so good, so arousing. His tongue tantalized her to the point where she quivered with excitement. A warm pool of pleasure had been eddying inside Amelia, but at that moment it came pouring out in a great torrent of hot desire. He suckled her other breast until she thought she might drown in delight.

In time, Fletcher knelt on the floor at her feet. Before she realized what he was doing, he smoothed his hand up her bare back and held her while his mouth traveled down her belly. Amelia writhed in his embrace, driven mad by the patterns he drew on her skin. His tongue felt warm and liquid, but her own flesh had turned searingly hot.

Amelia gasped, "Fletcher, I can't stand it."

"What do you want, love? Tell me."

She wanted to feel his tongue in all her secret places. She wanted him inside her, enveloping her, too.

"Tell me," urged Fletcher.

"Just—please, don't make me wait."

With his teeth, he unsnapped her jeans. Then he shot her another look—half amused, half carnal. "In a hurry?"

"Yes, please. I—I want you so badly."

"Then take off your clothes," he commanded, rocking back on his heels to wait.

Amelia laughed breathlessly. "Is this a demanding, macho side of you I haven't seen before, Fletcher?"

"Just get them off," he said darkly. "Unless you want me to tear something."

His expression was a hungry glower. Amelia kicked her boots off. "All right, but I'm putting you on warning right now. I won't let you tie me up, Fletcher. At least, not on a first date."

He laughed. "I'm just afraid I'll botch the job. I'm shaking too badly to undress you properly."

Amelia hadn't noticed that he was quaking as hard as she was. The sight of his aroused state was intoxicating.

Her socks went flying. Then she peeled off her jeans and reached for her panties. She thought she heard Fletcher groan.

Fletcher watched Amelia undress and wondered if he'd ever been so aroused in his entire life. She was a lovely combination of shy lady and excited, sensual woman. In the firelight, her fair skin gleamed like pearl. Her hair shone. Her breasts were full, her hips so beautifully curved that he couldn't keep his hands off her any longer.

"This much I can handle," he said, helping her ease the silky pink panties down over her thighs. Then he grasped her buttocks and pulled her close again. He soon discovered that she was ready for him—hot and melting inside. She threw back her head to gasp for breath as his intimate caresses coaxed her to a higher plane of excitement.

Amelia's face was even more beautiful in abandonment. Her eyes were hazy blue; her mouth was lusciously slack from his rough kisses. A delicate flush crept up her throat and colored her cheeks. Whether she knew it or not, she was a highly sexual woman. The idea of awakening her to the delights of lovemaking was exceedingly erotic.

"God," he said, raking her slender, trembling body with his eyes. "I can't wait to be inside you."

She sank down on the bunk at that, her lovely, naked knees parted ever so slightly. "I want you, too." Her voice was suffused with a soft hoarseness. Her eyes glowed with fearless anticipation—an invitation pure and simple.

Fletcher stood up and flung off his clothes. His entire body had begun to throb. He saw her smile as he tore off his underwear, and so he grabbed her shoulders as if to push her down across the bunk and take her then and there.

But Amelia refused to lie down. She perched on the edge of the bunk and without a word used her mouth and clever fingertips to bring Fletcher to the brink of ecstasy.

Later he couldn't remember what he said, but Amelia laughed at last and stretched out on the sleeping bag like a languid cat. She curled her long legs around his hips, wrapped her arms around his neck and blew a sigh of pure pleasure in his ear as Fletcher found his way inside her. In one long thrust, he buried himself in the warm softness of her body. At that instant, he reached her deepest core, her perfect center, the spot where her soul lay most vulnerable. Amelia responded with a quiet purr of satisfaction.

"Lady," he whispered, "where have you been all my life?"

Her musical laugh tickled his ear. "Oh, Fletcher, where would you be without your clichés?"

"They've gotten me this far."

"They have, indeed." She snuggled against him, drawing Fletcher even deeper inside herself. Her breasts burned against his chest, the hard nipples branding his skin.

He allowed that moment of pleasure to wash over him. Tightly plunged into a wonderfully sexy woman whose gaze had turned so murky blue, Fletcher wondered if he might get lost in those fathomless eyes of hers. She was a beautiful woman in many ways—sensitive and courageous, determined and sexual. How had he stumbled upon her after so many years of wandering?

"What are you thinking?" she asked so softly he almost didn't hear.

"That I want this to last a long, long time," he replied.

The urge to thrust within her was almost too compelling to ignore. But that would bring about a climax all too quickly. Fletcher forced himself to rock gently against her, and soon Amelia caught the rhythm and moved with him. It was magical after that—sometimes excruciatingly slow, then gradually building to a fiery tempo. Her mouth tasted sweet; her body felt delicious. She moved with him as if they'd been lovers for many years.

He wanted to give her great joy, but he couldn't hold back. And suddenly there was no need to. Instinctively he began to thrust harder and harder, and Amelia urged him on. She responded wildly, moving faster and then crying out with such abandon that Fletcher's heart swelled. Like a glorious primitive creature, she arched against him, pulsing and calling his name in a voice that sent Fletcher into the maelstrom of passion.

Their release came simultaneously in an intense explosion of incandescent fire. Fletcher held her hard against himself, as if by sheer strength alone he could sustain that perfect moment of climax. They drifted for a time on that wonderful plateau between reality and ecstasy.

Then, slowly, they returned to earth. A peaceful cocoon semeed to surround them, blocking out everything but that small room with the softly crackling fire and two human beings breathing as one.

Fletcher found the sight of Amelia's drowsy face next to his almost as heart stopping after lovemaking as it was during the act. He kissed her lush lips, rubbed her soft nose with his. Her smile sent tickles of excitement along his limbs.

"I don't want to go to sleep," she whispered after a long time, pensively caressing Fletcher's cheek with her fingertips. "I want this feeling to go on forever."

"How do you feel?"

"Like I'm glowing."

"You are, love."

"Fletcher—" she began, then stopped.

When Amelia didn't finish her sentence, he propped himself up on one elbow and looked down at her thoughtful expression. "What is it?"

She shook her head, tracing a line down his bare chest and watching her progress with great concentration. "Nothing. Maybe it's better this way."

"What way?"

"Never mind."

He touched her chin, tipping her face back to his. "Tell me what you're thinking. It can't be more intimate than what we've just done."

She smiled. "Sometimes it's easier not to talk."

He knew exactly what she meant. Talking meant bringing up the past—and the future. And Fletcher understood that there was no future between him and Amelia Daniels. Hadn't she said it a dozen times? Whatever demons had chased her away from the mountains hadn't been exorcised, and she wanted to get back to New York as soon as possible. Fletcher's life was tied completely to his land and his sons—the only possessions that were entirely his own. There would be no future between him and Amelia Daniels. Not in this lifetime.

She touched his face again, doubtless having read his expression too accurately. "Don't talk and don't think," she said. "Just kiss me, all right?"

Her lips coaxed him once more, and soon Fletcher's mind went blank again. There was only the luscious woman in his arms, making his heart beat fast with her teasing kisses.

When she pulled back, Fletcher was breathing raggedly. "Where," he asked on a husky laugh, "did you learn to kiss like that?"

With a grin, she said, "Correspondence school."

He laughed and settled back with her, tugging the edge of the sleeping bag up over her bare legs and deciding to keep the rest of her warm by himself. He smoothed his hand back and forth across her collarbones, enjoying the silky texture of her skin and the way her hair wisped around his fingertips.

As he watched, her eyes grew languorous under his caresses. Fletcher began to smile as her response grew more pronounced and he accused, "You told me you didn't like sex very much."

"I didn't say I didn't like it." She caught his hand just before he moved to cup her breast again. "I said I wasn't much good at it."

"That's clearly not the case."

"When I was married, I—well, we weren't a terribly sexual couple, I guess. He was much older than I was—a professor of mine, in fact."

"He admired your legs while you sat in the front row?"

Amelia smiled. "No, nothing like that. I worked as his assistant and helped him prepare his research. He was—is—a historian. We spent a lot of time in the library."

"That would have turned me on, all right."

She laughed. "Well, he suited me fine at the time. I had longed for—well, I needed someone who needed me, I guess. And Herb did."

"Herb the historian? Hell, this guy sounds more and more exciting every minute!"

"I wasn't looking for excitement then, Fletcher."

"What about now?"

She stole a look at him, her expression unreadable. "I'm not looking for anything. You know that. Except to find a way to make things work with my daughter, of course. What about you, Fletcher? We never talk about you."

He sighed impatiently. "There's nothing to talk about, that's why. One failed marriage, three kids who cause assorted trouble—"

"Tell me about your marriage."

With a shrug, he said, "It was one of those childhood romances that didn't work out. Patty and I knew each other in high school. When I enlisted, she wrote me letters and I wrote back." More slowly he said, "Her letters got me through a lot of garbage over there."

Amelia's hand crept up his chest, her fingers curling in the crisp hair there. "Did you get married when you were discharged?"

"No, when I was on leave. She met me in Hawaii, and we tied the knot before a justice of the peace—a couple of kids who hardly knew each other except on paper. Our first four years of marriage I spent in Vietnam."

"You were over there a long time."

He nodded. It had been a hell of a long time, and it had taken him even longer to get over it. Even now, years later, he still woke up from particularly vivid dreams, sweating and cursing and wondering if he'd lost his mind. But he'd had things better than most guys. Piloting helicopters that pulled wounded kids out of the jungle was important work, one job in which a soldier could feel he was doing something good. It wasn't something

Fletcher had felt he could walk away from when his first tour was up.

He said, "I stuck it out until I got shot the second time. Then I figured my number was up and I'd better go home. By that time, Jesse was born—conceived in Japan when I saw Patty for our first anniversary—and the twins were on the way."

Amelia's eyes sparkled with laughter. "For a couple who spent most of their time apart, you managed to have a lot of children." She slid her hand down to caress him. "You must have been a very sexy guy, Fletcher."

"We didn't waste any time when we were together," Fletcher said with a laugh. "Now I realize the sex made up for a lack of other kinds of intimacy we both needed. Anyway, we figured we'd better take steps to prevent ourselves from having our own football team, so I did the manly thing and had a vasectomy. It was the bravest thing I've ever done in my life, believe me—"

Amelia gasped, her eyes popped and her hand flew to her mouth. "Good grief, I never even thought about birth control tonight!"

Laughing at her appalled expression, he said, "Me, neither. Good thing I had the foresight years ago, hmm?"

"Dear heaven," Amelia said, blinking comically. "I've never forgotten that precaution in my life. You must have addled my brains, Fletcher."

"I'm glad," he said warmly, arranging her hair with his thumb. "I like a woman who loses her head in bed."

Amelia cast an inquiring glance at him. "Did Patty?"

He smiled, shaking his head. "She was as much of an amateur as I was when it came to sex. She read a lot of books and came up with some crazy stuff that was supposed to turn me on. Dressing herself in plastic wrap, decorating our bedroom like a house of ill repute—things that were basically inconvenient. I wasn't appreciative enough, I guess.''

"You didn't laugh at her, I hope?"

"Not really. But I couldn't convince her that I wanted her just the way she was—or had been. But she had grown up and still had growing to do. She wanted to go to school and see the world, and I wanted to have a home and get on with my life. We split up for a while—she went to California and I started building the ranch.''

"What about the boys?"

"They traveled back and forth for a while, but ended up spending most of their time with me. Then Patty met somebody else, and the boys hated him on sight. I agreed to the divorce as long as I had custody of the kids. She agreed to that immediately.''

Amelia looked surprised. "She didn't want to share custody?"

"Nope. The new husband is some kind of retail tycoon who has no interest in a family. She's happy with him, and I'm glad. We both got what we needed and came out of it relatively unscathed.''

"But you still have regrets. I can see it in your face.''

Fletcher nodded. "Sure, sometimes I think the marriage might have worked if I hadn't been so stubborn. But I needed to be here. These mountains have a power and serenity that keep me sane.''

Touched, Amelia said, "I know what you mean. It used to be that way for me.''

The sight of her drowsy eyes and beautifully rounded breasts was intoxicating. Damned if he didn't feel an urge to start all over again. He gathered Amelia into his arms and rolled her onto her back. She laughed deep in her throat—a deliciously sexy sound. Fletcher rode intimately against her, delighted to find how perfectly they seemed to fit together, how instinctively she molded into his body.

In a low voice, he said, "We weren't going to talk at all, remember? And here I am bending your ear."

Her body was warm and welcoming; her smile was playful. "We have a long night ahead of us. Unless you're planning to sleep, I don't mind having my ear bent."

"Let's do something with the rest of your anatomy." He kissed her throat and nibbled her there.

She wrapped her arms around his shoulders. "Like what, Fletcher?"

Still busy with her soft skin, he asked, "Have you ever heard of the Sugarplum Twist?"

She laughed. "The what?"

"It's something I learned in Bangkok."

"That's supposed to be a very decadent place."

"It is. Very, very decadent. Especially the neighborhood where I picked this up. Want to try?"

"Am I going to like it?"

With his lips already against hers, Fletcher murmured, "You're gonna love it."

Eight

Fletcher awoke the next morning feeling euphoric and extraordinarily well rested despite a night in which he doubted either one of them got more than four hours of sleep. Sleeping soundly, Amelia lay curled against him, her hair still caught in Fletcher's fingers, her knee wedged warmly between his thighs. She looked too deeply asleep to wake, he decided, though he longed to draw her from her dreams with sweet caresses. Carefully he slid out of her arms and rolled out of their makeshift bed.

Walking softly to avoid waking her, he grabbed up his clothes and headed for the door, planning to dress outside. The poor woman needed all the rest she could get, Fletcher decided with a grin, considering their night together.

He opened the door and slipped out into the cold morning air—and got the shock of his life.

"'Morning, Dad."

Jesse was sitting on the steps. And Fletcher was standing in the doorway buck naked, the picture of guilt. He almost dropped his clothes.

Jesse worked very hard to suppress a grin. "Sleep well, Dad?"

Clutching his clothes, Fletcher stepped outside and closed the cabin door behind him. He cleared his throat to make sure his voice didn't squeak. "What are you doing here?"

"Waiting for you," Jesse said innocently. He sat back and linked his hands behind his head, relaxed and amused. "I started wondering if you were going to sleep all day."

"What time is it?"

"Nine or so. Gosh, I never knew you to sleep so late. You must have had a busy night." Jesse watched as Fletcher dropped everything but his jeans and started to struggle into them. "Oh, don't bother getting dressed, Dad. Not if you're not ready, I mean."

"I'm ready, I'm ready."

Jesse grinned. "Grouchy this morning, Dad?"

"Not until I saw you," Fletcher growled, hustling into the rest of his clothes.

Languidly watching his father scramble with his socks, Jesse said, "I thought I'd come down here and see if you were lonesome or something, but I guess—"

"I'm fine," Fletcher snapped. "Keep your voice down."

"Sure thing." Jesse smothered a grin. "Need some help with your boots, Dad? Oh, you only brought one outside. The other one is still under the bed, maybe? Want me to go get it?"

He was already half-up, so Fletcher pushed Jesse back down onto the step. "Just stay where you are and tell me what the hell you're doing here."

Jesse shrugged. "Well, I came to get you for breakfast, but maybe we'd better have a talk."

Suspicious, Fletcher demanded, "About what?"

"Safe sex, Dad."

Fletcher lost his voice.

Jesse said, "It's a very important issue, you know."

Fletcher sat down heavily. "Safe sex? You want to talk about safe sex? Now? This minute?"

"Not safe sex for me, Dad. For you."

"See here—"

"Remember that day before I went off to college? You took me up into the hills to look for lost calves and while we rode around you talked about all kinds of stuff I should know before I left home. We didn't find any calves that day, strangely enough. That part was a little peculiar, I thought. But you said that day that anytime's a good time to talk about important stuff like sex."

"What are you getting at, Jess?"

"A guy can't be too careful, Dad."

"*You're* telling *me*?"

"Sometimes we all need reminders—you said so yourself. So I thought maybe I ought to remind *you*. I assume the same rules apply to everyone, Dad. You know—where girls are concerned."

Fletcher felt himself flushing a very deep red.

"I mean, it's your own business, right? That's what you told me. But a guy has to take responsibility for his own actions. If you want to bake a cake, you have to expect to break a few eggs—that's what you said."

Pained to hear his own clichés thrown back in his face, Fletcher began, "Jess—"

"I mean it, Dad. Do you carry contraceptives around? Because you can't count on the woman all the time. You have to be prepared to live with the consequences if you do something headstrong like—"

"Don't worry about it, all right?"

"Well, making babies isn't the only issue," Jesse continued stubbornly. "You told me that, too. Your own health is at stake. You can't be sure about anybody these days."

"I can be sure about some people," Fletcher said forcefully, hoping to put an end to the discussion.

"I hope you're right," said Jesse. "Now, there's just one more thing."

Fletcher looked at the boy warily. "What?"

Jesse said seriously, "You gotta think about commitment, Dad. I didn't raise you to have a good time with some sweet young thing and run off the next morning without a by-your-leave. Remember? That's what you told me that day we were riding around. And I think—"

"Jesse," Fletcher said severely, "what makes you think I need this lecture?"

Jesse took a deep breath. "Well, Dad, here's the big question. Are you taking advantage of a nice lady just to make yourself feel good for a little while? I mean, I hate to think you're a Good Time Charlie."

Fletcher buried his head in his hands and groaned.

Laughing, Jesse said, "I mean; you can't just love 'em and leave 'em, Dad. That's not very mature."

Fletcher started to laugh, too. "Shut up, will you?"

"Sure, Dad. Anything you say. I just thought I'd make sure you were taking care of business, that's all."

They looked at each other, giggling like a couple of kids. Fletcher actually felt like a kid at that moment—not like a father, but an equal who was capable of foolishness as much as the young man sitting next to him.

Wiping tears of laughter, Jesse said, "Nice black eye, Dad."

"Thanks," Fletcher retorted proudly. "My kid gave it to me."

"He must have a good right hook."

"Sure does. I taught it to him myself."

"I'll bet he appreciated the lesson."

That set them both to laughing again, and when Amelia stepped out onto the porch a few minutes later, they were giggling and wrestling on the steps like a couple of little boys. They both straightened up and stared at her.

She looked disheveled and sexy as hell, dressed in her jeans and shirt, but with her feet still bare. Her hair was a lovely mess, and she blinked drowsily in the sunlight. Her smile was sleepy and beautiful. The sight of her—a woman still warm from the bed where they'd made passionate love for hours on end—rendered Fletcher speechless.

Jesse turned around, blinked and goggled at her as though she were a sex goddess.

"Good morning," she said to both of them, both hands sliding down her hips and into the front pockets of her jeans in an unconscious gesture that was more sensual than a striptease. She leaned on the doorjamb with her dusky blue eyes filling with fond amusement. "What serious discussion are you two having this morning?"

They both burst out laughing again and couldn't answer.

Amelia felt strangely at home as she walked between Fletcher and Jesse up to her father's cabin for breakfast. She had finished dressing and brushed her teeth at the water pump, and was enjoying listening to father and son exchange friendly insults as they strolled beneath the trees.

When Fletcher wrapped his arm around her waist, she felt even more content. His easy grin reassured her they hadn't made a mistake last night.

Breakfast was cooking when they arrived at the cabin.

"Well, it's the two sleepyheads!" announced Amelia's father as they entered the cabin. He was drinking coffee from a chipped mug and pacing stiffly by the fire. "Zoe, look who's decided to join the land of the living!"

Zoe was busy at the stove and didn't turn around. "I see," she said.

Amelia heard the note of tension in her daughter's voice and realized at once that things were not as cheerful as her father was pretending this morning. She saw the cold gleam of his smile and instantly felt nervous.

Fletcher was either being dense or pretending not to notice that something was amiss. He rubbed his hands together hungrily, the picture of a man ready to satisfy his appetite. "This place smells terrific this morning! What are you cooking, Zoe?" He peeked over her shoulder at the sizzling skillets.

"Pancakes and sausage," she said shortly, then shot him a glare that could have sizzled Fletcher pretty thoroughly if he'd been standing any closer.

"Great! I'm starved."

Archly Zoe said, "What's the matter? Did you work up an appetite last night?"

"Ahem," Jesse murmured uncomfortably to Amelia. "This was the part I should have warned you about."

Fletcher turned to Amelia, too. "Mrs. Daniels, is there something we should get out in the open this morning?"

"No," she said at once, panicked by the idea. "Let's not."

"It might be a smart move."

"No, please—"

Over her shoulder, Zoe said, "You're not going to break any bulletins we haven't figured out for ourselves."

Amelia's head began to throb. She sank down onto the bench by the table and rubbed her forehead. "Oh, dear. I thought this trip was going to be a simple rescue."

Zoe turned, spatula in hand. Her face was contorted with anger. "There isn't going to be any rescue at all, Mother. I don't need rescuing—simple or otherwise."

"Darling," Amelia said, striving to be patient and very calm, "you've had your adventure. Now it's time to go home."

"You've had *your* adventure, too, is that it?" Zoe sneered. "What's the matter? Wasn't he any good in bed?"

"Zoe!"

Mildly Fletcher said, "How about if I cook?"

Zoe shoved the spatula at him. "Here. Let's see if you're any good at that!"

"Zoe, I want you to apologize at once!"

"What for? What did I do wrong?"

"You're being very insulting to Mr. Fletcher, who—"

"Who slept with my mother last night! If you think I'm going to forgive him for that—"

"Forgive him!" Amelia surged to her feet. "See here, young lady, I'm a consenting adult! It was my decision to make last night, and I made it all by myself, so—"

"Hey—" Fletcher started, looking wounded.

"All right, we *both* made it, but it was our business, not anyone else's."

"Great example you're setting, Mom," Zoe cracked. "I didn't think you were the type to sleep around."

"I'm not, and you know it! You are just using this to confuse the real issue here."

"There *isn't* an issue," Zoe insisted. "I'm staying here, and that's final. Granddad promised I could."

Amelia swung on her father. "Why in heaven's name did you do that?"

"Because it's true," said the old man. "She can stay here if she wants to."

"Forget it," Amelia snapped. "Hell will freeze over before I allow my daughter to live in this place with you."

"Better buy yourself a new coat then, girl, because I think she's staying."

"Why?" Amelia demanded, furious at the two of them for ganging up on her. "Why do you want Zoe? You were glad to see me go! Why start all over again?"

"She wants to stay. She likes the place, and I could use some help around here this winter. I'm getting old, and she's not bad company. If she wants a home, she's welcome to make it here."

"I forbid it," Amelia said flatly.

Zoe challenged, "How are you going to stop me?"

"I'm your mother!"

"So what?"

"The law is on my side, for one thing. You have to go to school, you know."

Zoe obviously hadn't thought of that angle before. "Well," she said, her lower lip puckering, "I could live down the mountain during the week and come up here on weekends. I could live with the Fletchers, maybe."

"Oh, no," Fletcher retorted. "Don't drag us into this mess. Not after the cracks you made to me this morning."

"I'm sorry," the teenager said anxiously. "I didn't mean it. I was mad at her and—and—it was just a thing to say, that's all. I can't go back to New York!"

Amelia grabbed Zoe's wrist. "You'll hate it here after a while, you know. It's a lonely place—no friends, no telephone. Why, there isn't even a car at the moment!"

"There will be," said Brook. "Once the lumbering is finished."

"How long will that be? Months, perhaps! What if you break your leg, Zoe? It's a day's ride by horseback before you could get to the nearest ambulance! This is a ridiculous place to grow up! It's not safe. It's—"

"You did it," Zoe accused. "And I want to try."

"No."

"I feel at home here, Mother!" Tears trembled in Zoe's huge blue eyes. Her voice broke. "If you loved me, you'd let me try, at least! Please!"

Amelia wanted to cry, too. "Oh, Zoe," she whispered.

Brook came to the table and sat down heavily. In the silence, he looked from Amelia to Zoe and back again. "How about a trial period?"

"What?"

"Let the girl stay here for a little while—long enough to get a taste of it. I'll look after her."

"He will," Zoe asserted. "I know he will, Mom."

"For how long?" Amelia asked slowly.

Brook shrugged. "How about a month?"

"Absolutely not!"

"Two weeks, then."

"The law says she has to go to school. They'll come haul you away if you're acting as her guardian and preventing her from attending."

He lifted his hands. "All right, give us a week, then we'll figure out where we stand. Maybe she'll be sick of me by then."

"I won't," Zoe said fervently, seizing his hand. "I promise I won't. Please, Mom, let me try. I can't go back to New York. I don't belong there. I have to be in a place I belong or I'll go crazy."

Where had Amelia heard that idea before? She looked to Fletcher, hoping for some help—some support.

He shook his head. "It's your call."

Amelia sat down unsteadily. She needed time to think—but wondered if she'd feel any different after weeks of consideration. She hated the thought of giving up Zoe even for a few days. It was too painful. She shook her head. "Zoe, I can't—I can't leave without you."

Zoe knelt on the floor and put her hands in Amelia's lap. Her upturned face turned very young and naive. "You could stay here, too, Mom."

Amelia laughed. "And do what? Pick blueberries and bake biscuits all day?"

"You could be a lawyer here. People need lawyers all over the place."

"No," Amelia said harshly. "I'm not going to live on this mountain again. My practice is in the city. I have to get back, in fact. I've got appointments scheduled for Monday."

"In that case, we'll have to talk on the phone a lot."

"There *isn't* a phone!"

"I could ride down to Fletcher's ranch once in a while. I'll bet he'll let me use the telephone, at least."

Fletcher nodded. "At least."

Amelia shot him a look. "You think she ought to stay here, don't you?"

He shrugged. "If she wants to stay, that's half the battle, right?"

Amelia closed her eyes. Nobody was on her side, and she felt terrible. A wave of loneliness swept over her at that moment.

"Can I stay, Mom?" Zoe asked in a small voice. "For a week, at least?"

"All right," she said quietly. "For a week. That's it."

Zoe hugged her hard, catching Amelia into her arms and squeezing for all she was worth. Tears clogged her voice. "Oh, thank you, thank you, Mom. I love you. I really do."

Amelia could hardly speak, but she forced herself. "I love you, too, darling." She hugged her little girl back and never wanted to let go.

Then she heard Fletcher's voice.

"Damn," he said. "I think I burned breakfast."

When the meal was cooked all over again—this time with Amelia and Zoe handling the kitchen duties—everyone sat down for a late breakfast. Fletcher watched Amelia indirectly. He knew she was suffering inside, and he wished he could take her into his arms and make her feel better.

But Zoe was watching him like a hawk, so he kept his distance. The kid was downright suspicious that he'd stolen her mother's virtue and intended to do nefarious things with it.

Brook interrupted Fletcher's thoughts by leaning on one elbow and asking, "What's your agenda for today, son? You heading back to your ranch today?"

Fletcher had planned to break the news more gently to Amelia, but he didn't have a choice. "Yes, that was my plan," he said. "I have to get back to my boys. They're expecting me."

Brook frowned. "You're getting a late start."

"The trip's mostly downhill from here. It won't take long to get home."

"I had hoped you might join me for a little mayhem today."

"Mayhem?" Amelia questioned, skewering her father with a narrow look.

Brook ignored her and concentrated on convincing Fletcher to stick around. "I thought I might give those lumber company fellows a scare."

"What kind of scare?" Amelia insisted on an answer. "What nonsense are you cooking up now?"

Brook turned to her, annoyed. "Just a little visit that might slow down the progress at the lumber camp a little. If I give them some trouble, they might decide that lumbering this area isn't worth the effort."

Uneasily, Fletcher said, "Maybe there's a better way to do that."

"Yes," Amelia said firmly. "All we need right now is for you to get hauled off to jail for harassing people who are only doing their jobs."

"You have a better idea, girl? Or don't you care what happens to this forest?"

"I care," Amelia replied, sipping her coffee with prim efficiency—a gesture that was obviously a sham to disguise her real emotion on the subject. "And I do have a better idea, if you're interested. Let me see the contract you signed."

"Why?" Brook demanded belligerently.

"Because I'm a lawyer," she shot back. "Maybe I can find a loophole."

"A what?"

"Something that we can use," Amelia explained, "to break the contract. My job, you see, is writing contracts that can't be broken, so I know what to look for."

"What have you got to lose?" Fletcher said to Brook.

Brook grunted. "It's worth a try, I suppose. Zoe, get into my desk over there and bring me the second drawer."

"The whole drawer?"

"Yes, dammit. Don't you understand English?"

Zoe took no offense and brought the drawer, which was jammed full of papers, magazines and stubby pencils. "This is a mess," she remarked. "How can you find anything?"

"Just hand it over," Brook growled. He pawed through the clutter for several minutes before coming up with a sheaf of legal-size papers. The pages had been closely typed, and the paragraphs were long. He pushed the document across the table at Amelia.

"Thanks," she said, and stood up. With the contract in hand, she turned to go.

"Hey, where are you going with that?"

"This will take a while," she said. "I'm going outside to read."

While Amelia sat on the porch and studied the contract, Fletcher decided to help Zoe wash the breakfast dishes in an effort to make peace with the girl. But she proved to be as stubborn as her mother and wouldn't say a word to him, which forced Fletcher to keep up a running monologue of inanities. She even stepped on his foot once and spilled a potful of cold, soapy water down his shirt.

Jesse was drying the dishes and watching the whole farce. In an undertone, he said to his father, "You'd better get out of here, Dad, before she decides to use the boiling water next time."

But Fletcher stuck it out—for what it was worth. Zoe didn't inflict any more physical punishment, but it was clear she had no intention of forgiving him for seducing her mother. Still, Fletcher figured he'd better keep trying.

Some shouts from outside finally drew their attention, and Fletcher heard Amelia call, "Fletcher! You'd better come out here!"

Drying his hands on a dishtowel, he stopped dead in the doorway. He was astonished to see the rest of his family riding up to Brook Tucker's cabin.

"Dad!" Jake shouted, flinging himself off his tired horse. "Are we glad to see you!"

Luke and Jake hurried up onto the porch, crowding around their father and bubbling like a pack of hysterical wolf cubs.

"You won't believe what's happened," Luke cried.

"It's really awful. You've got to do something right away, Dad," Jake chimed in.

"Hold it, hold it," Fletcher commanded. "Pipe down, all of you. What the hell is going on?"

Again they tried to explain at the same time.

"We were rounding up cattle just like you told us," Luke started.

"And we headed up to the west acreage," Jake blurted out. "We found a few steers and then got a real shock."

"Yeah, a shock!"

Fletcher could see that the boys had ridden hard. Their horses's heads were hanging, and the boys themselves looked exhausted and scared. It was easy to guess that they'd probably spent the night at the base camp and ridden like a band of Indians to Tucker's Mountain that morning to bring the news—whatever the hell it was.

"All right, calm down," Fletcher said. "What happened?"

"The pasture's all torn up and there's machinery parked all over the place," Luke said, getting to the point. "Some lumber company has already started cutting trees."

"Somebody's cutting timber on our land?"

Both boys nodded vigorously, and Jake said, "We told them they were on the wrong property, but they wouldn't listen to us."

"Wait a minute. You talked to them?"

"Yeah," Jake responded breathlessly, "but they just laughed at us and said we didn't know what we were talking about. I wanted to go home and get some guns to show we meant business, but this wimp—"

"I am not a wimp," Luke snapped. "Besides, Dad has the key to the gun cabinet, stupid."

"And I've told you a hundred times you're not to go near the guns!"

Jake looked furious. "Yeah, but those guys laughed and—"

"We came up here to get you," Luke interrupted, stating the obvious. "You've got to stop them, Dad. They're making a terrible mess of our land."

Fletcher digested the situation in a matter of seconds and threw the dishtowel onto the nearest chair. "Okay, I'll take care of it. You boys stay here for the day, understand? Those horses are beat, and you can make yourselves useful to Mr. Tucker."

"Yes, sir," they chorused, clearly thankful to have their father taking charge.

"Jesse," he went on, turning to his eldest, "I want you to look after your brothers and bring them home tomorrow, got that? I want you at the ranch by nightfall."

"Yes, sir."

"Brook," Fletcher said, turning to shake his host's hand, "thanks for your hospitality. Feel free to take any payment out of these boys in labor. They're not bad workers if you keep your eye on them."

Brook grinned. "Will do, Fletcher. I hope to see you again soon."

"Thanks. Amelia—"

When he turned to her, she lifted her stubborn chin and shook her head emphatically. "There's no need to say goodbye to me. I'm coming with you."

"What?"

She was already folding up the contract and tucking it into her pocket for safekeeping. "You heard me. I'm going, too. You might need my help."

"Amelia—"

"There's no need for me to stay here, anyway," she said, resolutely avoiding a glance at her daughter. Briskly she added, "I have to be back in New York soon. In the meantime, you might need a lawyer."

"I've never needed a lawyer in my life!"

"What about your divorce?"

"Patty took care of it."

"Well, there's a first time for everything. If you want me, I'm available."

Fletcher grinned, enjoying the light of battle shining in her eyes. She was ready for action, all right, and he was already starting to feel sorry for any lumber company official who stood in her way. "I'm broke, you know. I may not be able to pay you for a while."

She smiled up at him. "We'll figure out something, I'm sure."

Nine

Horses were saddled, food was packed, gear assembled and hastily strapped onto the backs of saddles. Amelia and Zoe said goodbye with resolutely dry eyes. Their parting made Fletcher uneasy. He thought they'd both handle the separation better if they really allowed their feelings to show, but he didn't voice his opinion.

He decided they'd make better time without a pack horse, so he and Amelia set off within the hour on their two well-rested horses. They rode down the mountain at a fairly quick pace, then bore off the path instead of heading for the base camp. They plunged through the trees for a while, then hit the recently lumbered area.

For the rest of the morning, they picked their way through the ruined forest. Once a pair of bighorn sheep leaped out of the brush and fled, and a few deer skittered out of their path, but for the most part, they were alone. Fletcher led the way, urging his horse carefully across the rubble of the devastated land. He was glad Amelia stayed close on his heels.

They stopped in the middle of the afternoon to rest the animals and eat a quick lunch. While the horses snoozed under the trees, they climbed onto a rock together and sat in the sunshine, eating the sandwiches that Zoe had hastily prepared.

"How much farther?" Amelia asked as they ate.

"I'm not sure," he said honestly. "Maybe a couple more hours, judging by what the boys said."

"Will we make it before nightfall?"

"Why? Afraid to spend a night under the stars with me, Mrs. Daniels?"

She shot him a wry smile while rearranging the lettuce in her sandwich. "If you're going to howl at the moon again, Fletcher, I'd rather you did it in the privacy of a bedroom, not open country like this."

He laughed. "I don't remember howling last night."

"Short memory," she retorted.

"Oh, yeah?" he challenged. "I've met a few lawyers in my time, lady, but none of them could plead a case the way you did last night."

"I lost my head for a little while."

"A long while," he said with a grin. "I didn't think lawyers were supposed to let go of their emotions the way you did. Aren't you supposed to be coolheaded? Always in control in the courtroom and out?"

"I don't remember my diploma saying anything about a cool head."

Fletcher finished his sandwich in one last, enormous bite and lay back on the rock to soak up the sun. He folded his arms behind his head under the brim of his hat and relaxed, appreciatively studying Amelia's silhouette above him. He particularly liked the way her sweater clung to her breasts. He wondered how easily he might slip his hands up under it to find out if she was wearing a bra or not.

But he controlled the urge and asked instead, "What kind of lawyer are you, anyway? Do you write lots of wills for doddering old men who lust after your body?"

Amelia looked down at him and wondered if a sexier man existed on the planet. She doubted it. With half-closed eyes, she remembered how magnificent he had looked without his clothes the night before. The firelight had made his muscles gleam and cast a delightful sparkle in his eyes.

Shivering at the delicious memory, she said, "You're the only old man who's lusted after me lately, Fletcher."

"Who's calling me an old man?"

"It was a figure of speech. Touchy, are you?"

He shot her an amused expression. "I''m young enough to make you beg for mercy, remember?"

"I don't remember begging."

"Short memory." He tipped his hat down over his face to shield it from the sun. "Come on, Amelia. Tell me what you do for a living."

She tried to drag her mind off the thought of Fletcher's attractively relaxed frame long enough to answer his question. "All right. It's not very exciting, really. I don't do litigation."

"No Perry Mason courtroom stuff?"

"No, I work for a very large law firm in Manhattan, where I mostly study contracts written by my colleagues for various corporate clients. We specialize in mergers, which can be very tricky."

"Sounds pretty dull, if you ask me."

"Well, I'm not flying airplanes in thunderstorms," she admitted. "Or chasing cattle on a galloping horse over rough terrain. But it's a living. I have regular hours, and my salary enables me to afford a comfortable life-style for me and my daughter."

"You like the work?" he asked from under his hat.

"Sure. It's challenging—a lot of number crunching sometimes, but I'm good at it. Do you know how exhilarating it is when you're the one person the boss turns to when there's a big problem that's got to be solved fast? I'm pleased when they hand me the tough assignments. It makes me feel good."

"You see yourself doing it forever?"

"I'm a long way from making partner, if that's what you mean. But I've got plans in the meantime."

"Ambitions?"

She smiled. "I guess you could call it that. I'd like to be my own boss someday, so I'm saving my pennies. I want to set up my own practice."

"How many pennies do you need for that?"

"In Manhattan? Tens of thousands of dollars—and that's just for a little office in a cheap building with a part-time secretary."

"Ouch." Fletcher took off his hat and squinted up at the clouds scudding across the sky. "Do you know how long it would take me to make ten thousand dollars?"

Amelia smiled. "It's important to me. I don't mind a few sacrifices here and there."

"Why Manhattan? Why not someplace cheaper?"

"It's my home. That's where my friends are."

Amelia let that simplified answer stand, but there was more. She had gone to school in the city, made an ever-widening circle of friends and made her home there.

She had her regular hangouts—the gym where she took an exercise class, the neighborhood restaurants she frequented, the park where she liked to read the Sunday newspapers, the bookstore that served cappuccino while the customers browsed. She had her routine—the subway, the office coffee break, lunch on the street sometimes, or the sandwiches from the deli downstairs, then work all afternoon and home by cab if the weather was terrible. Until recently, evenings had been reserved for her daughter. Then Zoe's girlfriends started coming around—a crowd of teenagers seemed to constantly sit around their kitchen table, combing one another's hair and painting their fingernails. Amelia resented them for intruding on her relationship with her daughter, but things change. Children grow up.

It was impossible to explain fifteen years of adult life in a few sentences. But Amelia knew her life in New York was full—busy and happy most of the time.

Fletcher gave her a speculative glance, obviously thinking about her answer to his question. "What kind of friends?"

Amelia laughed. "What's that supposed to mean? Fletcher, are you jealous?"

He ignored the question, asking, "How many of your friends are men?"

"A few. Lots, in fact. Most of the people I work with are men."

"Oh, yeah? Are *they* lusting after your body?"

"Some of them, yes. But I prefer to keep my love life and my career completely separate."

He considered that for a while, eyeing her with a glimmer of something sexy in his gaze. "Does that mean," Fletcher finally said, "that you won't sleep with me tonight after we've finished our business?"

Amelia grinned. "Maybe I'll keep you guessing on that."

Fletcher wrapped his hand around her wrist and effortlessly pulled Amelia down on the rock with him. He pinned her legs beneath his hard thigh and cradled the back of her head on his arm.

"I hate guessing games," he said, and swooped down to kiss her.

Amelia slipped her arms around his strong neck and kissed him back. Her lips parted, and Fletcher made a slow and lazy business of exploring the inside of her mouth, until Amelia released a low sound in the back of her throat. Although the sun beat down upon them, Amelia knew the heat she felt wasn't emanating from the sky. She surrendered to it just the same, relishing the liquid warmth that bubbled inside.

Minutes later, Fletcher drew back. Amelia sighed, content to be in his arms a little longer. It felt good just to lie in the sun together with no need for words. Gently he brushed her loose hair from her face. The tenderness of that gesture made Amelia's throat ache suddenly. With feather-soft fingertips, she touched the bruise beneath his eye. Although she watched his expression and he returned her gaze with an equally curious flicker in his eyes, Amelia couldn't guess what he was thinking.

At last he said, "I'm sorry about what happened with Zoe this morning."

Amelia forced herself not to wince at the mention of what had taken place. Voice strained, she said, "It's only for a week."

"Maybe," said Fletcher.

"It is," Amelia said sharply. "I won't allow her to stay longer that that. Not with him."

Fletcher hesitated, then said, "I have a feeling they'll be good for each other."

She snorted. "Nobody could be good for my father. He's too far gone."

"He just needs some attention. A little love might do wonders for him. You ought to understand that."

"What do you mean?"

"Something you said before—that you're like him in a lot of ways."

Amelia didn't want to talk about love or her father at that moment. She pushed Fletcher, saying, "I think we'd better get going."

"Amelia." Fletcher held her down on the rock. "Wait."

"I think we've talked enough."

"Then let's stop talking," he said softly. "Kiss me, instead. Touch me."

The temptation was too hard to resist. Amelia loved the sensations his lips evoked and couldn't stop herself from caressing the hard, lean lines of his body. Her hands fit so perfectly into the hollow at the small of his back. The heat of his skin burned through his shirt.

Without thinking, Amelia pulled his shirttail out of his jeans. Fletcher laughed against her mouth.

He rolled easily into the valley of her thighs and rode against her body intimately. Before she could think, he had pulled up the hem of her sweater and was seeking her breasts with his hands.

"Mmm," he murmured approvingly. "No bra."

"I didn't have time this morning."

"I'm glad. God, you feel good."

"Fletcher," Amelia gasped when he made contact, thumbing her nipples until they hardened appreciatively. "Fletcher, we can't make love here."

"Oh, yes we can."

"It's broad daylight."

He snapped her jeans open. "So what?"

She struggled to stop his hands from delving into her panties. "Somebody might come along and see us. I'm not that free-spirited yet."

"We'll work on it."

"Please, Fletcher!"

He propped himself up on one elbow, looking attractively aroused. "I thought some women got turned on by the idea of an audience."

"Not me." She managed to wedge her hands against his chest and push. "I like things very private."

"Where's your sense of adventure?"

"You saw most of it last night."

He was smiling. "Now that I think of it, you were plenty adventurous then."

"The Sugarplum Twist?"

"Did you like it?"

"I loved it, but give me time to recover. Let me up, please. It's time to get on your horse again."

He groaned in pretended anguish. "Lady, do you have any idea what it's like to ride a horse in my condition? I could hurt myself!"

"I'll make you feel better tonight, I promise. Now, let's ride, partner."

He dawdled before climbing on his horse again, slipping on his aviator sunglasses and adjusting his hat. But they were soon making good time down the hillside.

Fletcher cursed half an hour later. "The boys were right," he snapped. "Those bastards have crossed the creek onto my land. Look at this mess!"

The forest looked as if a gigantic egg beater had torn through, ripping up everything in its path. Thousands of trees had been felled and dragged away.

The lumber camp lay a few miles inside a box canyon. It was easy to find—they just followed the roar and scream of power saws cutting through timber. Using the sound as their guide, they soon came upon the men and equipment. The air reeked of gasoline fumes.

Fletcher urged his horse past a sputtering bulldozer, and Amelia followed close behind. They rode into the middle of the work area, and their arrival caused all the men to stop working. Perhaps half a dozen loggers put down their tools and came down to see what was going on.

One burly man in a yellow hard hat and a red plaid jacket strode importantly up to Fletcher's horse. "Say, pal, you and the missus could get hurt up here. We're working."

"This isn't my missus," Fletcher said laconically. "She's my lawyer."

"Good afternoon," Amelia said politely. "I'm Amelia Daniels."

As the puzzled man started to tip his hard hat, Fletcher asked, "Are you the bozo in charge?"

The man's face turned red and his hand froze on his hat. "Who you calling a bozo?"

Fletcher took off his sunglasses, revealing the black eye. Leaning on his saddle, he said, "If you're the boss, you're the bozo. You're on my land."

"Who the hell are you?"

"I'm Ross Fletcher," he drawled. "You're supposed to be cutting timber on Tucker land, not mine."

"The hell we are."

"The hell you aren't. You're about four miles in the wrong direction, boys."

The man in the hard hat glared at Fletcher. "Our company surveyed this land last spring."

"Well, your surveyor obviously can't find his own behind with both hands!"

Amelia cleared her throat. "What Mr. Fletcher is
trying to say, gentlemen, is that you're going to have to
move your equipment off this land immediately."

All the men began to buzz at that news. "What the
hell—?"

"If you don't," Amelia continued calmly, "we'll contact the sheriff at once and petition the court to im-
pound everything as proof that you've trespassed."

One of the loggers said, "What's she sayin', chief?"

Amelia raised her voice. "I'm saying that we will seek
restitution for the damage you have willfully caused here.
This land is very important to my client. Not only does
it provide his livelihood, but it's his home and his life. To
see it destroyed has no doubt caused him great pain and
suffering. We believe we have no recourse but to sue in
the amount of two million dollars."

"Two million—?" Fletcher echoed, looking just as
shocked as the men on the ground.

She didn't bother to explain that the two million figure was much higher than the settlement she expected to
reach after long negotiations. To the logging chief, she
said, "If your company shows good faith, we may be
willing to settle this matter out of court, but until I am
contacted by the company's attorneys, I think it's only
prudent for you men to clear off this land as quickly as
you can."

"But—but—"

"Of course," she added sweetly, "we could call the
sheriff and ask that you all be arrested on the spot."

"Wait," cried the logging chief. "Don't do that!"

He agreed to stop the work on the spot, then hurried
off to supervise the moving of equipment. Fletcher

elected to stick around to make sure they did as they promised. They dismounted and rested their horses, watching the loggers scramble and talking over the din of roaring engines.

In less than two hours, they were following a convoy of trucks and bulldozers down the logging road cut through the pasture. A few cattle peered out of the brush to watch the noisy procession. They reached the highway and rode their horses along the shoulder of the road. A handful of cars and pickup trucks whizzed past.

The logging chief escorted them to a motel several miles up the highway. The place functioned as the boarding house for the loggers and a headquarters for the chief. Amelia used the motel phone to break the news to a lumber company vice president that he should get ready for a dandy of a lawsuit.

The vice president groaned at her description of what had taken place and said, "It was bound to happen sooner or later. We'll get back to you, Mrs. Daniels."

She gave him the phone number of her office.

"Oh, lord," said the vice president. "Fletcher's even hired a lawyer from New York? We're dead."

After the phone call they took their horses half a mile down the highway to a farm. A boy who lived there promised to look after them for the night.

"You're Jake Fletcher's dad, right?" the kid asked. "Jake's in my homeroom."

"Don't hold that against us," Fletcher said.

The boy grinned. "Sure thing, Mr. Fletcher. They'll be here in the morning for you."

The boy's mother gave Amelia and Fletcher a ride back to the motel in her pickup truck. Amelia was thankful for the lift. The lack of sleep and full day of horseback riding had started to catch up with her. She could see that

Fletcher was tired, too. She offered to treat him to a steak dinner in the motel's honky-tonk bar.

Taking the last available table—one right beside the jukebox—they ordered food from a gum-cracking waitress. The noise of other patrons, a television tuned to a football game, and the blaring jukebox prevented much conversation. Being with Fletcher was enough to make Amelia relax, however, and he seemed to unwind a little, too.

"You were great today," he said to Amelia over T-bone steaks and fluffy baked potatoes. The hubbub of the restaurant swirled around them. "Don't tell me that reading merger contracts is more exciting than having a showdown like the one this afternoon."

"Today was different," Amelia admitted. "It was a good feeling to be able to use my degree to protect something I really care about for once."

"So," Fletcher said, planting one elbow on the table and leaning close, "you care about this land, after all, Mrs. Daniels?"

"You know I do."

His dark gaze rested on her thoughtfully. "I think you belong here, Amelia."

With a laugh, she said, "Oh, no, I don't! This is lonely country, Fletcher. I like being around lots of people."

"It doesn't have to be lonely."

"But it usually turns out that way."

"Amelia—"

She stopped him quickly. "Forget it, Fletcher. Don't try to change my mind on this subject."

His face tightened. Amelia saw at once that he had intended to try. Maybe he had planned to say a few things she had even longed to hear, too. But she had shut him up too fast.

"I'm sorry," she said, suddenly afraid of what could happen between them before she went back to the city. She shook her head. "I know where this conversation is going."

He said, "You're not even willing to try?"

"Fletcher, you and I—" She caught herself.

His gaze was intense. "We're good together, lady. Very good."

"Maybe sometimes, maybe for a little while, but—" Amelia set down her silverware, suddenly not interested in food at all. "Can't we just enjoy what we've got?"

"What have we got?" he asked coldly.

Amelia swallowed the sudden lump in her throat, hardly able to look at him. "One more night together."

"And then?"

"Then I go back to New York, where I belong, and you go back to your ranch."

"It doesn't have to be that way."

"I think it does. And if you understood me better, you'd see that I'm right."

He took a breath, ready to argue the point. But they were interrupted at that moment.

One of the loggers who had been shoving quarters into the jukebox suddenly hunkered down over Amelia's shoulder and said, "How about a dance, honey?"

Amelia jumped, startled by the man's touch. His flushed, beery face was so close that she drew back in distaste. He was young—barely twenty-five, she guessed—and unkempt as well as rude. She recognized him as one of the loggers on the crew they'd just chased off the mountain. His breath smelled of beer and mint candies. "Thanks," she said, trying to be polite. "But not tonight."

"Aw, come on, baby!" The young man began to pull on her arm. "Just one dance. You're so pretty!"

"Leave her alone, pal," said Fletcher.

The loud music prevented the drunk from hearing the note of warning in Fletcher's voice.

"Just one dance," he begged. "One dance. Come on. It won't kill you!"

His buddies had been leaning over the jukebox and turned to watch their friend tug Amelia's arm. They laughed at his antics, swigging beer from bottles and lounging against the machine. One of them cheered.

"Please," said Amelia, trying to diffuse the situation by being quietly firm. "Let me finish my dinner, all right? Then we'll see."

"No, no, right now, baby. Let's do it!"

Fletcher rolled to his feet, took one pace and dropped his hand on the drunk's shoulder. His grip must have been stronger than it looked, because the young man released Amelia's arm and swung around, startled and angry. Fletcher held his ground, and his face—complete with blackened eye and two days' worth of stubble— looked very dangerous, indeed.

But the kid didn't notice. He shrugged off Fletcher's grasp. "Hey, get your hands off me!"

"Leave the lady alone," Fletcher growled.

The drunk made a crude suggestion, and his buddies burst out laughing.

Fletcher shrugged, willing to let the insult pass. "Go bother somebody who'll listen."

"I don't want nobody else," the young drunk said, squinting at Fletcher through bloodshot eyes without really noticing that Fletcher was at least four inches taller than he was. "I want her! You got something to say about it?"

Fletcher sighed. "Listen, son—"

"Go take a walk," the young man snapped impatiently. "Better yet, let's you and me take a walk together, man. Let's go outside and see who gets to take this pretty lady home tonight."

Amelia stood up hastily. She saw something dangerous flicker in Fletcher's eyes. "Ross, don't. It's been a long day."

"Damn right, it has."

She put her hand on his chest. "Please. You're angry with me, not him."

The drunk grabbed Amelia's elbow and twisted. She cried out as he shoved her aside and stepped in front of Fletcher. "Hit me, man," he taunted. "Hit me, I dare you!"

At once, his friends surrounded them—all bristling for a fight. The rock-and-roll song on the jukebox died away, leaving the restaurant suddenly silent.

Quietly, but unmistakably meaning every word, Fletcher said, "Listen, son, you throw a punch in here, you're not going to walk out, you understand?"

"Quit talking and hit me, man! Just try it!"

"This isn't the school playground," said Fletcher, his voice going even softer. "And you won't be standing when it's all over. Not you, and not one of your little friends, either. I will hurt you."

His last words were not a statement but a promise.

The young drunk blinked. Finally he heard the undercurrent of menace in Fletcher's voice and saw the deadly expression on his face.

One of the young man's friends said, "Hey, Lonnie, give the guy a break."

"Yeah," said another voice. "Let him eat his dinner."

The drunk glared around at the circle of his friends and ended up shrugging with a sneer. "Aw, hell. There are prettier girls around, anyway."

Amelia laughed at the remark, but something must have snapped in Fletcher. Quick as a striking snake, he reached out and smacked the young man across the side of the head. It was a whalloping reprimand, a blow so fast and hard that Amelia cried out. The young man fell against the jukebox, knocked for a loop. He lay there for a stunned second, holding his face and staring up at Fletcher in astonishment. Everyone froze.

The drunk blinked. "Sorry," he whispered, unable to tear his gaze from Fletcher's hard expression.

"Say it to the lady," Fletcher commanded.

Never taking his eyes from Fletcher, the kid said, "I'm sorry I insulted you, ma'am. I didn't mean it."

"That's better," said Fletcher. "You had enough, Amelia?"

"Yes," she said weakly, and allowed him to take her arm and propel her out of the restaurant.

They took a room at the motel for the night. It was a far cry from the Waldorf—rather a cheap, tacky place with a burned-out neon sign on the highway and twenty rooms, each with its own parking space outside. The desk clerk shot terrified looks up at Fletcher the whole time she processed their dinner bill and found them a room key.

Without speaking, Fletcher led Amelia around back of the building and unlocked their door. He went inside first and flicked on the lamp.

"Another night of luxury," Amelia said lightly, examining the room as she followed him inside. There was one double bed with a purple coverlet, a laminated dresser, a television set and a swivel chair with flowered padding.

It was the bed that drew her attention, of course. Suddenly Amelia wasn't sure she wanted to spend the night in it with Fletcher. Sleeping in drafty cabins had been one thing, but this seemed too civilized—too much like real life. And up until now, making love with Ross Fletcher had felt more like a fairy tale than reality.

"Not exactly the honeymoon suite," Fletcher replied. He closed the door and caught sight of her face. "But I guess the honeymoon is over, anyway."

"Fletcher—"

"I'm going to take a shower," he said, cutting her off. He turned away, already unbuttoning his shirt.

"Fletcher, please—"

"We've said everything we need to say, Amelia." In one motion, he tore off his shirt and the T-shirt underneath and threw them on the bed. "I need to cool off."

He went into the bathroom and closed the door. Amelia sat on the edge of the bed and tried to force her brain to function. No use. Either she was too tired to think straight or she didn't want to think anymore. In a moment, she heard the shower start to run.

Without thinking, she reached for his shirts and pulled them into her lap. How had everything gone so thoroughly wrong? Why did she feel like such a rat for choosing to go home where she belonged?

She looked at the telephone and considered calling someone back in New York. But who? Who would believe everything that had happened so far? Her straitlaced feminist girlfriend Frieda would be appalled that Amelia had fallen into even a nodding acquaintance with a man as demanding as Fletcher. And her officemate Joanne, the one who went alone to Mel Gibson movies dozens of times, would want to know all the gory details. Neither response was what Amelia wanted. She longed for a friend at that moment—someone comfortable who wouldn't be horrified by what she'd done or laugh at her for not doing more.

Feeling very alone, she put her face into his shirt to hold back the tears that threatened to spill from her eyes.

Then the bathroom door opened just enough for Fletcher's head to poke out. Amelia straightened immediately, hoping he hadn't guessed how miserable she felt.

"Hey," he called softly. "This shower's big enough for two."

There was a ghost of a grin playing on his mouth, but his eyes were full of understanding.

Without hesitation, Amelia stripped off her clothes and joined him.

He had scrubbed his hair and was rinsing it under the shower when she stepped in and pulled the rubber shower curtain behind her, closing them both in a world by themselves.

She hugged him hard from behind and rested her head on his broad back. "I'm sorry about dinner."

He turned in her embrace—wet and soapy and very naked. Then he seized her tightly. Against her hair, his voice sounded strained—whether from exhaustion or tension she couldn't be sure. "If we get hungry later, we'll call room service."

She tried to laugh. "Do you suppose anyone at this place has ever heard of room service?"

"Surely they'll send up a bag of potato chips if we ask nicely enough."

"Let me do the phoning," Amelia said, lifting her trembling mouth to be kissed. "I have a feeling that word has gotten around about you, cowboy."

He kissed her gently at first. Gradually their lips and tongues began to grind together hungrily. Amelia's whole body ached for more, and she found herself clinging to Fletcher for dear life. Steam curled from the streaming water, wreathing them in a strangely comforting mist.

"I want to take care of you, Amelia," he murmured.

Amelia smiled unsteadily. "I don't think I can cope with the kind of care you took in the bar."

"I'm sorry. I should have handled that kid a little differently."

"You certainly know how to get results."

"Not always."

Fletcher reached for a tube of shampoo provided by the motel and began to wash Amelia's hair. She closed her eyes and let the warm water cascade over her naked body while Fletcher soaped her hair with gentle hands and pressed wet kisses up and down the back of her neck.

Soap-slick and sensual, his hands slid over her breasts and belly while he murmured to her, telling Amelia how beautiful she was to him. She began to feel wonderfully revived and cleansed—both inside and out—as he lathered her body, then swept her under the warm spray so the clear water rinsed the soap away.

She wanted to take care of him, too, and rubbed the soap thoroughly into the hair on his chest, then glided her slippery hands out along his glistening shoulders, down his belly and around the taut muscle of his buttocks. She memorized the more subtle shapes of his body, too—first with her hands, then with her mouth. Her lips and tongue drew circles all over his wet skin.

Fletcher didn't speak, but his breathing changed to tight gasps as she slipped her knee between his legs to part them and cup the prize she found there. He leaned against the shower wall and groaned, his hands playing erotic games with her breasts. His passion-lazy gaze burned into hers as they caressed and teased each other to the point of near climax.

Finally he pushed her hand away and took her into his arms again. "There's a perfectly good bed in the next room," he murmured against her earlobe. "And this might be our last chance to use one."

Attempting to smile, she said, "I won't know how to behave on a real mattress."

Fletcher shut off the water. "We'll think of something good."

She took her time drying him off with a thick white towel, and Fletcher was very careful to dab her all over and behind the ears before wrapping her hair up in the last dry towel. Amelia found her legs were trembling then.

"Fletcher," she said, holding on to him for support, "there are lots of things I feel we ought to say to each other right now."

"Let's not." He caught her into his arms and lifted Amelia off her feet. "I don't want to hear any more words."

He carried her into the bedroom and deposited her on the bed. Amelia pulled down the covers and drew Fletcher by the hand into the cool sheets with her. He pressed her down into the bed, and she arched against his hard body, relishing the tension she felt vibrating in him. He was pulsing and ready for her, and there seemed no reason to postpone what they both wanted. In an instant, he was inside her.

They lay locked together for a long time, letting their hearts beat the message that their minds would not allow them to communicate. Her hands trembled on his shoulders. She could feel Fletcher's arms quivering in response as he held her tightly against himself. Then Amelia found his mouth with hers and kissed him. She nibbled his chin, rubbed her cheek along the rough stubble of his jaw and bit gently into his ear.

"I love to hold you," she whispered. "I love to feel you against me."

"And inside?" he whispered back. "Do you love me inside you?"

"I love that, too."

He withdrew for an instant, then thrust into her again—higher this time and finding his way very slowly. "Do you love this?"

Her voice caught in her throat as intense sensations shot up through her body. "Yes."

"And this?" he asked, touching her most sensitive spot with his fingertips. Massaging her tenderly, he brought all of her senses alight. "Do you love this, Amelia?"

"Oh, yes."

"And this?" He slid down to caress her with his mouth, teasing Amelia with his clever tongue until she panted and writhed beneath him.

"Yes, yes!"

He knelt above her, poised to enter once again and holding her inescapably against the bed. Then he asked, "What don't you love, darling?"

She dragged her eyes open and found his intense gaze holding hers. Her heart began to pound. "Fletcher—"

"What don't you love?" he asked again, suddenly rough as he plunged inside her once more. "Tell me, Amelia."

The powerful thrust sent a wonderful surge of pleasure all the way to her throat so that she cried out. "I love it all," she gasped. "I love everything you do to me."

"Everything?"

"I love your touch. I love your voice." When he buried himself deep inside her again, Amelia cried, "I love *you*, dammit!"

With a hoarse groan, he quickened his rhythm. Each plunge sent Amelia closer and closer to the edge of ecstasy. She wrapped her legs around his hips, meeting each thrust breathlessly. Then abruptly he slowed the pace, deliberately witholding the final pleasure.

"Do you love me, Amelia? Really?"

"I can't help it." She knotted her fists against his chest and squeezing her eyes tightly shut to hold back the emotion that threatened to break through. "It's all wrong and it would never work, but I love you."

"It's not wrong. You just can't see how right it is."

"We'd be terrible together, Fletcher."

"We're good, damn you!"

"We have good sex," Amelia argued. "It's hot and it's wonderful, but it's not enough. It can't change things—not for me."

Fletcher cursed and rolled away, abandoning her. He sat up and swung his long legs over the edge of the bed.

Amelia scrambled up and put her hands on his bare back. "Listen to me. I do love you, but I can't come here and be with you."

His hunched shoulders were very tense. "What's so damned terrific about New York?"

"It's not the city—it's me. When I'm there, I'm my own person. Don't you get it? I need the city the way you need these mountains."

"What are you talking about?"

"I'm not Brook Tucker's daughter or even Zoe Daniels's mother or—or Ross Fletcher's lover. I'm *me*—the person I created—the complete woman I want to be.

I can't live in somebody's shadow again—I'd go crazy. There's too much history for me here."

"Bull. You're just afraid to try."

"The memories are too painful."

He grabbed her shoulders. "Don't talk to me about painful memories, lady!"

"I'm not as strong as you are!"

"The hell you aren't! Your father made you strong, whether you like it or not—strong enough to break out on your own, get yourself a damn good education and find a job in the toughest city in the world. If you can make it there, you can make it here."

"I *have* made it there—I've spent all my life getting what I want! I can't throw it away and start all over again."

"Because you're afraid you might fail?"

"Yes! I'm scared to death I might lose it all and end up where I started—trapped on that damned mountain again!"

"We're all trapped, Amelia. We choose our traps and learn to love them—kids, work, lovers. And I love you so damn much, lady!"

He must have realized how hard he was gripping her, because he relaxed his hold at that moment and remorse filled his eyes. Softly he said, "Amelia, I'm not your father. I don't want to make you unhappy again. I need you."

Emotionally spent, she leaned against him. "You don't need anything but your sons and your ranch."

"That's not true." He eased her back into the bed once more, kissing her tears and cradling her in his arms. "I'm in love with you and I want to be with you. You've brought something into my life I never had before."

He gave up trying to make sense and tried to convince her with his lips, his hands, his body. She resisted for a while—fighting off the passion for as long as she could hold out. Fletcher coaxed and teased, pushing her to the edge of her senses. But gradually she gave in, her conscience swept away on a torrent of hot love. Her hands found their way to each rugged muscle of his back, his chest, his hips. He was so strong and perfect, and he urged her with such reverent insistence that Amelia surrendered to him completely.

When her climax came, the sensations nearly exploded inside Amelia, rocketing her to a sublimely wonderful place light years from the present. She wept, arching upward until Fletcher's hoarse cry of release echoed her own and they floated blissfully in each other's arms.

He didn't speak again, and Amelia didn't attempt to break the silence, either. More words would have spoiled things, she knew. And she wanted to keep the moment perfect—the better to remember it.

She slept after a while, and spent the night dozing fitfully. Fletcher slept badly, too. She felt every move he made—every sleepy mutter and tightening of his embrace. She awoke early and listened to him breathe for a while, making up her mind. At last, she slipped out of Fletcher's arms, careful not to awaken him.

She dressed quietly, then stood for a long time at the edge of the bed, watching him sleep and wondering what might have been. In time, she gathered herself together and left.

Ten

When Fletcher awoke in the morning, Amelia was gone. He knew it before he was fully conscious. She had run away from him—paying for the motel room before she left, of course and leaving a check for his services as pilot and guide. Unerringly polite to the end.

He took his horses and went home. The boys returned the same day. They spent the afternoon rounding up cattle and another day driving them into town. It was hard work, but Fletcher was glad to have it. It was good to have something to concentrate on.

He thought he was keeping his mood a secret, but maybe he didn't do such a great job of it. He began to notice that the boys gave him a wide berth, obeyed every command with a snappy "yes, sir!" They did their chores without being told. Jake even went to school without complaint.

On the first evening he was at home, Jesse asked to be allowed to return to Tucker's Mountain.

"Brook said he could use a hand around the place for a few weeks," Jesse explained. "He might even pay me."

"That'd be unusual," Fletcher cracked. Then he relented a moment later. "Sure, go ahead. Look out for Zoe while you're up there."

He surprised the hell out of Jesse by handing the boy a bottle of beer from the refrigerator. Fletcher was pretty sure his son had been sneaking a few now and then with his friends, but this was the first official drink between father and son. Jesse took the bottle and tried to look nonchalant about twisting off the cap.

"Zoe doesn't need looking after," he said after a quick sip. "It's her granddad I feel sorry for. She's bossin' him around something terrible."

"Don't waste your sympathy." Fletcher drained most of his beer in several swallows. "Just be glad there's no female bossing you around down here."

"Yes, sir," said Jesse doubtfully. They finished their beer in broody silence.

Jesse left the next morning, the other boys went to school and Fletcher went to town to cash Amelia's check for services rendered and the check from the market, too. He put the money on his loans to appease the bank a little longer. They seemed delighted to take his cash.

He tinkered with his plane after that and spent a hell of a lot of time wondering about women.

He got home in time to cook spaghetti and meatballs for the boys but managed to forget to stir the pasta, so most of it ended up in a glob at the bottom of the pot. Fletcher cursed a blue streak when he discovered the mess. The boys assured him the meal was fine, choked it down without a single complaint. They dispersed quickly after the meal to do—so they claimed—their homework. They tiptoed around their father for the rest of the evening and went to bed early.

At midnight, when Fletcher was in bed not sleeping but staring at the ceiling, the telephone rang. He stumbled down the stairs in his underwear, muttering, "Who the hell is calling at this hour?"

He knew as soon as he picked up the phone and heard the static on the line.

"Fletcher?" Amelia said when he didn't speak. "Did I wake you?"

Damn it all, but the sound of her voice could make any man weak as a kitten. The knot in his stomach loosened, and his heart did a complete turn in his chest. He sat down on the sofa in the dark, gripping the receiver as if afraid it might jump out of his hand like a thrashing trout. "No," he said when he could breathe again. "You didn't wake me."

She sighed in his ear, a soft sound of relief. "I was afraid you weren't going to say a word. I—I owe you an apology."

"Yes, ma'am, you do. You could have kissed me goodbye, at least."

"I did. You even mumbled something, but I didn't understand all of it. Something about scrambled eggs."

He did not laugh. "I woke up hungry."

She was silent for a moment, then said slowly, "Fletcher, I—it's good to hear your voice. I missed you these past few days."

"Days? It feels like months."

She hesitated again, and suddenly he was afraid she was going to hang up. To keep her talking, he asked, "Where are you?"

"My apartment. My—my bed." She cleared her throat. "I'm wearing your T-shirt, as a matter of fact."

"I wondered what happened to that."

"I could pretend I picked it up by accident, but that would be a lie. I stole it on purpose."

"That must mean you don't hate me."

"I don't hate you, Fletcher. I—well—" Amelia coughed and said a little stronger, "Look, the reason I called is your lawsuit."

He leaned back into the sofa, pulling the phone with him. "I never had one of those before. I suppose it's some kind of status thing in New York."

"Nearly every self-respecting citizen has one," she replied, forcing the lightness into her voice. "I started the paperwork, made a couple of phone calls on my lunch hour."

"Does your boss know? I don't want you to get into trouble over this."

"They'll never hear about it. It's small potatoes."

"If it's not worth your time," he started sharply.

"No, no, please don't misunderstand. I—I just wanted you to know that everything's in motion. I've made an appointment for a conference call with the lumber people on Thursday. I think I've got my father's situation nearly sewn up and yours isn't far behind."

"I guess that's good news."

"Yes. I also telephoned a friend I have in an admissions office in Boston. She's going to send some information to Luke about scholarships. It's a good school and not too overwhelming for a boy his age. They have a special program for accelerated students."

"Boston, hmm?"

"My friend and I are having lunch this week to talk. Maybe by Friday I'll have something concrete to tell you on both subjects."

"You could call before then just for the hell of it. I don't mind listening to you breathe."

She laughed, then hiccuped strangely. "Oh, hell," she said. "This isn't going well at all, is it? Maybe I should hang up."

"Don't do that," Fletcher said quickly. "Please, Amelia."

"Oh, Fletcher," she said, then gave a sigh that ended in an awful gasp.

Desperate, he said, "Amelia, everything I said still goes. I love you."

She inhaled deeply and said, "I know."

He growled in frustration, damning the miles that stood between them. "So why aren't we together?"

"I explained all that, didn't I?"

"Not to anyone's satisfaction but your own!"

"Fletcher—" Her voice cracked and broke. "I fought too hard against that mountain to give up now. My life is here. My friends, my job." She tried to laugh, but it came out a choke. "My—my dry cleaner, my hairdresser, my—"

"Stop. I can't compete with a dry cleaner."

"The point is that I belong here."

"No," he said. "*Half* of you belongs there."

"Fletcher—"

"Face it, Amelia, you're not a whole person in New York. Part of you is here with me. Until we're together, you're not complete. You're still an unhappy woman who's looking for herself."

"Stop, please."

"Don't be like your father, Amelia—shutting out love because you don't know how to deal with it."

"Is that what you think I'm doing?"

"I don't know. We need to talk. You're coming to get Zoe at the end of the week, right? Will you come here for a couple of days on the weekend, please? I've got to see you."

"I'm not coming, Fletcher."

"Please, I'm going crazy, Amelia!"

"I'm not coming." Crying for certain then, she said, "I've reserved a plane ticket for Zoe. She can pick it up at the airport."

"What are you talking about?"

"I can't see you. I—I hope you'll take Zoe to the airport for me. I'll pay you, of course."

Fletcher cursed. "You take your damn money and—"

"Please don't be angry. I'm right about this. It's for the best."

"The hell it is," he said. "I'm coming to get you. I'll fly out in the morning—"

"No, you won't. I'm asking you not to, Ross."

"That's supposed to stop me?"

"Yes, it is. I don't want to see you. And I know you'll respect that. I'm asking you not to come, Ross. Please."

There was no more to say. Fletcher sat for a long moment in stunned silence. Then he hung up the phone. For an hour, he stayed downstairs in the dark. The telephone did not ring again.

Jesse spent the rest of the week doing odd jobs for Brook Tucker. On Saturday, he got up early to escort Zoe Daniels down the mountain to his father's ranch. He was surprised when Brook announced he was riding along.

"I'd like to talk to your old man again," he said to Jesse as they saddled horses. "He's not a bad fellow."

"He's crazy at the moment," Jesse muttered.

"Oh?" Brook frowned speculatively and said no more.

When they arrived at the ranch that evening, they were greeted by Luke and Jake, who announced that their father was spending the night in town after flying a party of lumber company executives around the mountains all day.

"Be glad he's not here," Luke said when they were all sitting around the kitchen table playing a halfhearted game of poker. "I'll tell you, Jesse, he's nuts."

"Yeah," Jake added. "He hasn't said one stupid cliché all week. Hell, he's hardly *spoken* all week."

"He's in love," Luke said dolefully.

Zoe sat up suspiciously. "With who?"

"Your mom, jerk. Who else?"

Zoe kicked him under the table, then frowned. "She was acting pretty weird, too. And it wasn't just because of me. Granddad, do you suppose she could—"

"Be in love, too?" Brook shrugged, studying the cards arranged in his hand. "It's possible. She wasn't going to fall for the first man she met, but I figured she'd fall hard when the time finally came. Maybe something's happened between them. Maybe she's being stubborn about it."

"What d'you mean?" Jake asked.

"She probably doesn't want to come live here with your pop. And he certainly can't pack up and move to New York. It's a standoff."

"They're being stupid."

Everyone around the table agreed and played one hand of poker in silence. Zoe won, which pleased nobody—not even her. Jake dealt another set of cards around the table, but nobody picked them up.

Jesse slammed his fist on the table. "There's got to be a way to bring them together."

Luke nodded. "Exactly what I was thinking. Maybe I could call her with some questions about college."

"That wouldn't get her to come back, would it? We need a way to trap them together so they can work it out."

Jake sat up excitedly. "Hey, great idea!"

"I could call her," Zoe suggested slowly, enthusiasm catching on. "I've been pretty lonesome for her. I could tell her I broke my leg. That would get her on the first plane."

Jake jumped in with another idea, but Jesse stopped listening. He watched as Brook Tucker got up from the table without a word. In the doorway to the living room, he looked back and motioned Jesse to follow. Jesse got up and trailed Brook into the next room.

"What's up?"

"Help me figure out how to use this damn-fool telephone," Brook commanded. "I think I'll call my daughter."

Jesse grinned, pulling the telephone out from under a pile of Luke's geometry homework. "What are you going to say?"

"I'll think of something to get her here."

On Saturday night, Amelia did her grocery shopping at the market around the corner from her apartment building. It seemed strange to be buying only enough food for herself. After she paid her bill, she decided she wasn't hungry enough to go to the trouble of preparing a meal. She took a walk around the block, then another, hoping the exercise might cheer her up. It didn't.

Dispirited, she lugged the grocery bag up two flights of stairs and heard her telephone ringing when she arrived on the landing. Her heart leaped at the sound. She nearly dropped the bag as she struggled with her key, but managed to rush into her kitchen in time to grab the receiver off the wall before her caller gave up.

"Hello?"

"It's me," said the voice on the other end of the line. "Your father."

Amelia couldn't breathe for an instant. "Is it Zoe? Something's wrong?"

"Nothing's wrong with Zoe," he assured her. "She's fine. A little lonely for you, but that's all."

She had never heard her father's voice on the telephone before. He sounded uncertain and far away. But before her heart softened toward him, Amelia realized why he was probably calling.

"Zoe cannot stay any longer," Amelia said at once. "It's time for her to come home."

"I'm not calling about Zoe," Brook said.

"She didn't ask you to call me?"

"No, I'm talking for myself."

Amelia set her bag of groceries on the counter, suddenly bewildered and a little scared. A silence stretched on the line until she said, "This is the first time you've ever called me." Her voice trembled. "I can't imagine what you want to talk about."

"The lumber company thing," he said gruffly. "Some lawyer of theirs came to see me this week. He said you were trying to make trouble with my contract."

"That's right. I think I found a loophole. That's what you wanted, right?"

"Well, this young fellow said I should sign a new contract."

"Don't do that," Amelia said at once. "Heavens, that means we've got them on the run!"

"Well, he's coming back on Monday. I think they're going to try to make me sign something."

"Don't do it."

"What if they make me?"

"Who has ever made you do something you didn't want to do?"

"Sometimes," said Brook obscurely, "people do things on the spur of the moment."

Amelia listened to the next silence for a while, biting her lower lip and thinking. "Dad," she asked finally, "what are you asking?"

He harrumphed and coughed and finally answered. "I think maybe you ought to come back and give me a hand. I could use your help, Amelia."

She felt a lump rising in her throat and couldn't speak for a moment. "Do you know," she said at last, "that's the first time you've said my name in twenty years?"

"There are a lot of things I should have said, I suppose. But I thought—well, I never did know how to handle you after your mother died." More softly he added, "I figured it would be better all around if I shut up and toughened you up. It worked, you know. You grew up fast and did pretty well on your own."

"I'm not so sure."

"I'm proud of you. Your mother would be, too."

She couldn't breathe and couldn't speak.

"You had a hard childhood, but you turned out okay," he went on. "I taught you everything I knew, and you learned the rest on your own. But there's one lesson we both missed. And that's about needing love to make everything else worthwhile.''

His voice began to shake, but he continued, saying, ''I loved your mother more than anything in the world. And when she died, I thought my life was over. I took my anger out on you, I guess.''

''I loved her, too.''

''I know you did. And we made a mistake not pulling together when we needed each other. Maybe you were too young to try. It wasn't until your Zoe got up here and started pushing me around that I realized what you and I missed together.''

Amelia smiled shakily. ''She's a strong-willed girl.''

''She's a good girl. I love her a lot.''

Amelia's eyes blurred with tears as she heard her father say, ''I love you, too, Amelia. And I need your help right now. I wish you could find it in your heart to forgive an ornery cuss like me and—and—''

''I'll come,'' she said softly. ''I'll come tomorrow, if you like.''

''I'd appreciate it,'' he said. ''I'd like to get to know you again. Come home, Amelia.''

Eleven

On Sunday morning, Fletcher snoozed in his rusty chair at the back of his hangar outside Missoula. He'd spent a long night not sleeping and didn't feel up to facing his family just yet, so he propped his boots on the desk, folded his arms across his chest, pulled his hat down over his eyes and tried counting sheep.

After a while he heard a car pull up outside. He intended to ignore it, but he couldn't ignore the sound of somebody opening the hangar door and crossing the cracked concrete with quick, sharp footsteps. High-heeled footsteps.

Then her perfume filled his head, and Fletcher nudged his hat up far enough to take a peek.

Amelia stopped on the other side of the desk. She was wearing her business suit again—that sophisticated jacket and a short skirt that should have elected her legs a national treasure. Leaning down, she laid her hands on the blotter and looked at him with a half smile on her lovely mouth. Her blue eyes were full of warm light and the faint sheen of tears. She said, "A man at the gas station across the road said I could hire a plane in here."

He sat up slowly, half afraid to hope, half afraid to make any sudden moves for fear the dream might evaporate. He said, "Depends on where you're going, lady. This plane doesn't fly just anyplace."

"I need a ride to Tucker's Mountain. You know where that is?"

"Yeah, sure." He took a deep breath to steady himself and asked, "How long are you staying?"

She shrugged casually. "A day or two. It's too isolated up there for me for very long. I need a place with a little more civilization."

Fletcher could hardly speak for the pounding in his chest. "How much more?"

She smiled, and bright tears flooded her eyes. "Oh, I'd like a place with a phone, at least. A real bed would be nice. And I need a place to put my desk. I'm a lawyer, you see. I thought I might open up a practice out here. I understand there's a need for good legal help in this area."

"There's a need for a lot of other things in this area, too." He got to his feet, longing to rush to her side and grab her into his arms. He forced himself to be calm, saying, "But some people aren't cut out to live in this country."

She nodded. "I heard that's true. But I grew up here, you see. I think I know what I'm getting into."

Fletcher took her into his arms, and Amelia immediately wound her arms around his neck. He pulled her close, and her body melted against his as though they'd never been apart.

"Lady," Fletcher said, his voice turning husky, "I was afraid I'd never see you again."

"I couldn't stay away." She drew his head down to kiss him, and her lips tasted sweetly salty. She whispered, "I was hard on you, Fletcher. I'm sorry. I had things to work out."

"With your father?"

"I didn't understand his point of view. But he—well, I think there's hope for us yet. I'm here to try, anyway."

"And Zoe?"

"I think I can make her happy, too."

"They're not the only reasons you've come back, I hope."

"No, they're not." She was trembling in his arms, but said in a strong voice, "I was angry with my father for years, but I could still function. Without you, though, I couldn't. I was miserable this week, Fletcher."

Laughing, he said, "You don't know what miserable is."

She touched his cheek. "I think I do. I could hear it in your voice. I can see it in your face. I'm sorry I put you through this, Fletcher."

With a grin, he said, "You'll make it up to me."

"I'm going to try."

When she kissed him, he felt an overpowering emotion encircle them. Amelia must have felt it, too, for she gave a quiet little gasp and poured her soul into the kiss. Fletcher held her fast and rejoiced. She was back, this tough, stubborn woman with a heart as soft as a feather pillow, and she was willing to be his. He had never experienced such an intense surge of pure joy as the wave that nearly knocked him over at that moment. He leaned against the desk, pulling her with him and seeking to pull her slender body closer yet. He wanted to be a part of her and make her his forever.

She started laughing against his mouth and grabbed his shoulders to keep her balance. Their bodies clung together with an unmistakably erotic charge flickering between them. "God, Fletcher," she said, breathless and smiling when they drew apart again, "I love you."

"I love you," he said, chest tight with emotion. "Marry me, Amelia."

His words startled her, but that didn't last. Amelia read the pleasure in his dark, sparkling eyes and knew he wanted them to be together as much as she did. She had packed up and left New York believing that she wasn't going back except to move her belongings and settle business matters. She knew where she wanted to spend the rest of her life.

"Are you sure you want me, Fletcher?"

"My love, I can't get along without you. I need you desperately." He traced the curve of her smile with his fingertip—a gesture that made her heart turn over. "Can you stand living with me in a houseful of teenagers?"

"They'll be gone too soon, you know. We'll enjoy them while they're with us. And," she added, "we can always send them to my father's place for a weekend."

"Good idea. But although I'm rich in children," he cautioned, "I'm financially broke, you know."

"Not for long," she countered, pleased to be bringing good news. "I think it's safe to say that we'll be able to live quite comfortably at the ranch while your sons attend very expensive colleges."

Fletcher's grin was wide. "Am I going to marry a very sharp lawyer, Amelia?"

"Yes," she said, accepting his proposal warmly. "You most definitely are."

"Hot damn." He cupped her face and swooped down to drown her senses in a kiss that was long and sweet. His body was warm and reassuring, but arousing, too. While his mouth teased hers, he slipped his hands down her back and lifted her against his hard frame. With a sigh, Amelia wrapped her arms around him and didn't let go.

When the kiss broke, she found Fletcher's eyes warm upon her and smiled. "Think we can get a justice of the peace to climb the mountain?"

"I'll hijack one if that's what it takes. I want to marry you up there—on land we're going to share for a long, long time."

"We're going to be happy, aren't we, Fletcher?"

"Very happy. I love you, Amelia."

She snuggled against him once more, sure in the knowledge that she had come home.

*   *   *   *   *

EXTRA ROMANCE THIS CHRISTMAS FROM SILHOUETTE

SILHOUETTE CHRISTMAS STORIES – £3.50

Four short romances, specially selected for their festive themes, in one seasonal volume.

CHRISTMAS MAGIC –
Annette Broadrick
THE TWELFTH MOON –
Kathleen Eagle
EIGHT NIGHTS –
Brooke Hastings
MIRACLE ON I-40
Curtiss Ann Matlock

Available in your shops from 12th October, 1990.

SILHOUETTE CHRISTMAS PACK – £6.00

Four brand new Sensation novels in an attractive gift pack make an ideal Christmas treat for yourself or a friend.

MRS SCROOGE –
Barbara Bretton
STRANGERS NO MORE –
Naomi Horton
A CAROL CHRISTMAS –
Muriel Jensen
ROOM AT THE INN –
Marilyn Pappano

Look out for the pack from 26th October, 1990

Two special treats that combine the magic of Christmas and the romance of Silhouette.

Available from Boots, Martins, John Menzies, W.H. Smith, Woolworths and other paperback stockists.

Also available from Reader Service, P.O. Box 236, Thornton Road, Croydon, Surrey, CR9 3RU.

NOVEMBER TITLES

SLOW BURN
Mary Lynn Baxter

LOOK BEYOND THE DREAM
Noelle Berry McCue

TEMPORARY HONEYMOON
Katherine Granger

HOT ON HER TRAIL
Jean Barrett

SMILES
Cathie Linz

SHOWDOWN
Nancy Martin

COMING NEXT MONTH

CANDLELIGHT FOR TWO
Annette Broadrick

Jessica Sheldon and Steve Donovan were related by
marriage yet they shared nothing except mutual
dislike. The man was gorgeous — but totally
insufferable! The last thing Jessica needed was
Steve's 'brotherly' escort around Australia; it was
much too dangerous!

NOT EASY
Lass Small

Ruggedly appealing, determined, bossy, persistent
— they all described Winslow Homer. He was a
sweet-talking chauvinist who had never met anyone
as infuriating as Penelope Rutherford. She was
adept at avoiding predatory males, but there was
something about Homer …

ECHOES FROM THE HEART
Kelly Jamison

Brenna McShane had never forgotten her very sexy
— and unreliable — ex-husband. What was she
going to do now that Luke McShane had returned,
bringing home all the remembered pain … and all
the remembered passion of their young love?

Silhouette Desire

COMING NEXT MONTH

YANKEE LOVER
Beverly Barton

Laurel Drew was writing her ancestor's biography when big, blond and brawny John Mason showed up with a different story. Sparks soon began to fly between this Southern belle and her Yankee lover.

BETWEEN FRIENDS
Candace Spencer

Catherine Parrish had waited a lifetime to hear Logan Fletcher propose. But now that Logan had asked her to marry him, he asked because Catherine was his friend and not for romantic reasons. Why, once they were married, did their old friendship seem to elusive?

HOTSHOT
Kathleen Korbel

Devon Kane was the archetypal rolling stone. He'd photographed world leaders, rebellions and disasters, always hopping from one plane to another and never making commitments. Then he was sent to do a photo-story on Libby Matthews; what was she hiding and did it affect them?

4 SILHOUETTE DESIRES AND 2 FREE GIFTS
- yours absolutely free!

The emotional lives of mature, career-minded heroines blend with believable situations, and prove that there is more to love than mere romance. Please accept a lavish FREE offer of 4 books, a cuddly teddy and a special MYSTERY GIFT... Then, if you choose, go on to enjoy 6 more exciting Silhouette Desires, each month, at just £1.40 each. Send the coupon below at once to: Silhouette Reader Service, FREEPOST, PO Box 236, Croydon, Surrey CR9 9EL.

YES Please rush me my 4 Free Silhouette Desires and 2 Free Gifts! Please also reserve me a Reader Service Subscription. If I decide to subscribe I can look forward to receiving 6 brand new Silhouette Desires each month for just £8.40. Post and packing is free, and there's a Free monthly newsletter. If I choose not to subscribe I shall write to you within 10 days - but I am free to keep the books and gifts. I can cancel or suspend my subscription at any time. I an over 18. Please write in BLOCK CAPITALS.

Mrs/Miss/Ms/Mr _____ EP99SD

Address _____

_____

_____ Postcode _____

(Please don't forget to include your postcode)

Signature _____